Love of the Boss

Kayla Olsen

Contents

CHAPTER 1: What A Party.....NOT!

V ARIELLA

Tonight I was looking forward to as it happened to be our one month anniversary that he told me he wanted to celebrate by going to a party that a good friend of his invited him and me to.

Normally, I don't do parties. However, I figured that it wouldn't hurt since I'd be with him anyways.

So once I agreed to go, I asked my one of my coworkers to cover my shift at the strip club I work as a waitress at. My best friend, Morielle, is a stripper there and is really good too. In fact, I think she's one of the best dancers there and wish I had her figure and her confidence. Mainly her confidence especially about her body. I'd love to have that with my body.

For the whole day, I just relaxed and treated myself to get pampered to help prepare myself for tonight and buy a nice dress for tonight along with a mask. He told me it's a masquerade but the masks we have to wear are supposed to be nice and fancy. So I buy one at a place that sells great quality costumes and accessories where Morielle usually goes to for her stage costumes.

Thankfully he had one that went with my dress and was a laced nice black one that had some things draping down it a little.

So I had my make up done all smokey eye and then light red lipstick along with my hair curled and pulled to the side over on one shoulder. Then right as I finished tying my mask on, I heard a knock on my apartment door and grabbed my clutch purse before opening it. It was my boyfriend.

"Wow, you look good." He comments.

Okay so it's not hot but I'm a curvy girl and he's the only guy that hasn't minded being with me.

I was feeling a little anxious actually because I felt like a masquerade type of a party would be fun and I had always wanted to go to one.

When we pulled up the long driveway in front of the house and got out, I was amazed at how big it was. It looked nice and as soon as we began walking inside after the two doormen opened the doors up, I became instantly more nervous as I started to walk alongside with my boyfriend, Blake with his hand behind my back as I noticed that there were a bunch of people in the room that some women were wearing black short dresses and matching masks as well as while the men, including Blake wore the same masks that were decorative in a manly way but were all the same color and all.

People in some places were standing around in a circle watching something and as we walked to the first circle to see what was going on, I was shocked when I noticed what this party was. It was just like the movie Eyes Wide Shut. Everyone came here to have sex with people.

Then the more I looked around the more I saw some other women wearing masks that were fully nude. Oh my god, why did he bring me here?

Suddenly I felt more uneasy and started to excuse myself by slipping through the crowd.

Once I got several feet from the front doors, I felt somebody grab my wrist roughly and turn me around to face them quickly. It was Blake.

"Where the hell are you going?!" He asks pissed off.

"I'm leaving. How the hell could you bring me to a party like this? I'm not a whore." I snap at him.

"Yes you are. You're my whore. And you're lucky to be with a guy like me. I mean seriously, look at you. You're fat and ugly and don't get many offers. At least this way people already paid and can't get a refund. So when it's our turn, you're gonna do what as I say and I'm gonna let everybody know you are mine." He says.

"So you want to screw me in front of strangers so they would know I'm yours?! I won't fucking do it you sick asshole!" I tell him.

"You don't say no to me! Besides, you said you wanted to make me happy and this is shat will. I want all the men to know you're mine and that I fuck you so good that they don't need to bother." He says while pushing me hard up against the wall.

Unfortunately we are in the darkest corner of the room so nobody can see us and they can't hear us as they are all busy going to all the crowded areas to watch the sex show.

"No." I tell him and am able to not knee him too hard but hard enough in between his legs to let me go and grab onto his crotch area.

"Fucking bitch!" He yells and that's when I start to run as fast as I can and not knowing this place and the fact it's huge, I notice that nobody is upstairs, so I quickly run up there as I see him not too far in the crowd coming towards the stairs.

When I get to the top of the stairs, I catch myself luckily as I lose my footing and almost trip from my heels and hurry to run towards the first door I see hoping it's unlocked. Which thankfully it is.

I run inside and quickly shut the door and lock it behind me. Then I turn around and notice the lights are on but I don't see anybody here.

Then I suddenly start hearing water coming from inside of the bathroom. Which of course judging by the size of the house I'm sure all of the rooms I bet have their own bathrooms. It's like a hotel in here.

Oh right, I need to try and call for a ride. However, as soon as I take out my phone, I notice it has no bars.

"Fuck!" I say under my breath.

I start looking around and don't see a telephone anywhere until I notice a cell phone on the side table by the bed. I hope he has better service since it looks more expensive than mine. So I walk over and grab the phone and hope that there's no code to get inside it.

Though right as soon as I am about to try and figure it out, I quickly get turned around roughly by the arm and harshly pushed up against the wall, causing me to drop the phone.

"What the hell are you doing in my room?!" This man with an angry killer kind of a look on his face tells me as he shoots daggers at me through his eyes.

"I-I'm sorry. I was trying to look for a phone to call for a ride." I start to tell him terrified.

"But why in here?! Why the hell in my room?! I don't like sluts from downstairs to come in my room to fuck!" He says as his grip on my wrists are getting tighter.

"Please. I'm not a whore. I was tricked into coming and I." I started to try and explain while hiding tears but then I heard a knock at the door, it was Blake. His voice on the other side called my name.

The man holding me against the wall glared at the door and then looked back at me while scowling. Then back again at the door before letting go of my wrists.

"Go in the bathroom and be quiet." He tells me and still shaking with fear, I do as he says and try holding in my tears.

Was this guy really gonna help me? Or was this a trick? And was he really just wearing nothing but a towel? Oh my god his body and tattoos are so hot.

'Oh my god, shut the hell up Variella!' I tell myself in my head.

I next hear the guy opening the door.....

CHAPTER 2: The LAST Thing I Need!

D ARIUS

"Please Mr. DeLucca. I swear I'll never be late on a payment again." The man that owes a huge debt to me and has been late on payments begs.

"Pff. You must have me mistaken for some other dumb ass who's more lenient. You KNEW before you made a deal with me the rules and what all the consequences were if there were no payments. So now, you have to suffer the consequences." I smirk at him.

"But Sir, I told you..." He began trying to explain once again that he has had a family emergency. Here's the thing though, this guy uses way too many excuses. So now, all that's left to do really is make an example out of him.

I take out my brass knuckles and begin throwing punches at him. Every blow is harder than the last. Teeth are flying out, blood squirts and then finally, the man is no longer breathing.

I might have a lot of his blood on my clothes and such but I needed to make an example out of him. I have a reputation to protect.

Afterwards, I decided to head on home and take a shower before passing out in bed. Although it became clear right away when I pulled up in the driveway that there was obviously a party going on.

My cousin I know was the one who started this. Luckily he's leaving tomorrow and as much as I love him cause he's family, sometimes I wish he wouldn't be such a dick in throwing one of his usual parties. I swear it's like a high school party with all the sluts and the alcohol except they're adults and he prefers throwing 'sex' parties.

I ignore it as long as everybody knows that upstairs is off limits. There's been too many incidences where skanks have come walking into my room either drunk or wanting to fuck me because of who I am. I never do that and besides, I have a booty call, Shanelle, to come and help out with those types of needs.

So I get out and go in through the back where I say 'hi' to a few of my guys guarding the backside of the house before I head inside and up towards my room.

I take a shower and toss my clothes in a bag like usual to have them taken care of later by one of the guys and scrub off all the blood.

For a moment I stand in the shower underneath the water as it cascades down my entire body. All while thinking about what I do.

Yeah, most wouldn't think I do things like that but I do. I always wonder about what else I could be doing if I wasn't do this as a career. Fuck it, I can't start thinking like that. I'm so tired. So I shut off the water, slick my hair back and tie the towel around my waist then as soon as I open the door, there standing just several feet away from me, was a curvy dark haired tall woman and she looked to be trying to use my phone? What the fuck?! That's when I start stomping my way up to her.

I then quickly turn her around roughly by the arm and harshly push her up against the wall, causing her to drop the phone.

"What the hell are you doing in my room?!" I demand angrily at her. I hate people coming into my room randomly without my permission.

"I-I'm sorry. I was trying to look for a phone to call for a ride." She started to tell me while terrified.

"But why in here?! Why the hell in my room?! I don't like ANYONE, especially from downstairs to come into my room without an invitation first!" I seethe through my teeth while I tighten my grip on her wrists that I'm holding together.

"Please. I was tricked into coming and I...." She started to try and explain while hiding tears, I noticed, but before I could say anything else, we heard a knock at the door. I then heard the one person who I would love nothing more than to teach him a lesson, Blake. One of my biggest enemies at the.moment. His voice on the other side called a female's name that I'm assuming is this bitch's name.

I continued holding her against the wall as I glared at the door and then looked back and scowled at her. Then turned my attention back again at the door before letting go of her wrists after she had even more fear in her eyes after Blake said her name.....She's lucky I hate this fucker.

"Go in the bathroom and be quiet." I tell her and still shaking with fear, she does as I tell her to and closes the door behind her. Then I see she left her purse on the inn table beside my bed and quickly hide it under my pillow before I start making my way towards the door to answer it.

The moment I swung opened the door abruptly, there standing right in front of me was a pissed off Blake.

"Where is she, Darius?!" He asks.

"Where's who?" I asked to fuck with him.

"Don't you play dumb with me." He says all smug.

"Listen, I don't know why you're here but I can promise there's nobody in here. So if you value your life at all, I suggest you get the fuck out of my house and think twice before ever stepping foot on my property ever again." I warn him with my arms crossed.

He looks me up and down scowling. Then I notice him sniffing the air a little.

"She's not in here huh?!" He says tongue-in-cheek.

"That's what I said." I glare at him back.

"Then why do I smell her perfume?" He asks.

"Not that it's any of your business, but I did have some girl leave here a few minutes ago." I tell him.

"Yeah, right." He says while trying to come in but I stop him by pushing him back.

"I ain't gonna tell you again, get the fuck off my property, or else." He says.

"Or else what? I'm not afraid of you." He tells me.

I look behind him and notice my guys walking up the stairs towards him and give him a nod.

"Take this piece of shit and teach him a lesson in why he shouldn't come back." I tell them as they roughly grab him and start dragging him downstairs towards the back to do what they do best.

Then I close my door and turn around to start walking towards the bathroom but stop half way when I notice the bathroom door open and out comes the girl.

"T-thank you." She says nervously. "I'm sorry I caused that to happen I just..." She began but I stopped her.

"Forget about it. He's being taken care of. So now would be a good time to leave." I tell her.

"Right." She says before she starts to head out.

Next chapter will be posted soon! :)

Alright guys, starting to post chapters for this one and the 'My Crush Is A Porn Star!?' Also, I will be posting sneek peeks for a few stories coming in a couple of weeks that I think you'll like. :):) Hope you liked this chapter. :)

CHAPTER 3: VIP Room

- -

V ARIELLA

Last night was eventful to say the least. Not to mention disturbing and frightening all at the same time. For a moment there I had thought maybe I was gonna get hurt by that guy who ended up saving me. Little did I know exactly who he was until later.

It wasn't until my alarm woke me up and I reached over to my little inn table beside the bed that I realized I didn't have my phone.

I sat up real fast and before getting up to look for it, I began thinking of what could have happened to it. Then it hit me, I left my purse at his place. Oh shit.

Oh my god this is bad. I didn't have a credit card in there or anything. Just my phone, my Drivers License and some cash. Oh shit, if he see's my information, he'll know where I live. I am so dead. Literally.

I start to place my hand over my chest as I feel it tightening while the panic sits in.

"Oh my god. What did I do?!" I started saying to myself out loud. "Please god don't let him find me and kill me. Just let him destroy it. I can always replace a phone."

Then I was startled as I heard knocking at the door. I realized that it most likely was Morielle. Since I didn't call her or nothing.

So I head to the door and before opening it, I ask who it is.

"It's the guy whose room you barged into last night." I hear that sexy deep voice say.

Wait! He isn't sexy. He's a killer. A criminal.

"H-how did you find me?" I asled although I immediately face palmed myself as I already knew was because I had left my purse.

"You left your purse in the room. Look, I'm a busy guy and took time out of my day to stop by and drop this off, can you at least let open the door so I can give it to you?" He asks.

Should I? Do I want to? Or should I just tell him to leave it by the door. Why the hell don't I have a bat by my door?!

"Uh, yeah. Just a second." I exclaim and quickly look around to try and find anything that is a weapon but the closest is on the kitchen and he seems to be getting impatient by the second.

"I'm not gonna stand here all day." He says, rather rudely.

"Okay." I reply and start to unlock the door then open the door up slowly.

The more I opened the door the more I caught a good look at him and his body as I notice he's doing the same thing with me. Next I notice my purse in his hand.

"Thanks." I tell him while trying to grab it before I shut the door. However he stops my hand.

"Can I use your bathroom?" He asks.

"Uh..." I start to think.

"I came a long way and I have to go." He tells me.

"Yeah, okay. I guess it's okay." I agree.

After all, this guy could most likely kill me with one hit. I point to where the bathroom was and he looked at me for a moment and walked closer to me, hands me the purse before making his way there.

When I hear him shut the bathroom door, I walk into the kitchen and start to breathe and let out the breath I hadn't realized I was holding in. I then looked at one of the kitchen knives and quickly turned around and kept my hand in close distance from it without making it too obvious as soon as I heard his voice come from behind me.

"I wouldn't do that if I were you." He says.

"Do what?" I try and play dumb.

"I'm not stupid. I know you're afraid of me due to my reputation. But don't worry, I won't hurt you. In fact," He begins to say while slowly walking towards me.

Then he stops halfway when we hear my door open and I see a man who looks to be dressed just as nice as him.

"Boss, we need to start heading towards the meeting." He says.

"What did I say?! Stay in the car and if you need to tell me something, then text me. Don't just barge in here!" He snaps at the guy.

"Sorry boss." He bows his head and starts closing the door.

"I'll hit you up later." He says while nodding his head.

"Please don't." I say under my breath but of course with my luck, he heard it.

"What was that?" He asks.

"I said, please don't." I repeat. "In fact, I would appreciate it if you forget all about my address." I tell him.

"I'll think about it." He winks at me before heading towards the door to leave.

The moment he closed the door and left, I slumped down onto the kitchen floor leaning against the cabinets and began trying to make sense of what all just happened.

I can't believe who was here in my apartment.

Next I heard my cell phone go off and I stood up and took it out of my purse and saw it was from 'Darius'. Oh god, should I answer it? And how the hell did he figure out the code to unlocking my phone to put in his number?

The phone goes off a couple more times and I block the number because I'm sure he probably would have texted me next. Now I won't have to worry about it.

Honestly I do feel a bit better knowing that I won't have to worry about him again.

Next I get ready for my waitressing job in my somewhat short black skirt with fishnets, heels, makeup done and hair doen and curly before heading there.

When I arrived and after clocking in, I headed to the back to put my purse in one of the employee lockers and coming right behind me was my best friend, Morielle.

"Hey girl!" She greets me as always all smiley and happy to see me.

"Hey." I replied.

"So what happened last night? You never told me about if you got home okay or not, bitch." She teases.

"Sorry. My phone died." I lie.

"It's cool. So was the party fun?" She asks while sitting down in front of her vanity mirror, fixing her makeup.

"Not really. It was more of a sex party." I tell her.

"What the fuck?! Are you serious?" She asks.

"Yeah. But it's okay, I dumped him." I smiled at her.

She screamed in excitement as she jumped up real fast and hugged me.

"Oh my god! It's about damn time." She says.

"I know." I laugh a little as she changes into another costume.

"Well, I need to head out there. I'll talk to you later." I tell her.

"See ya later." She says.

Once I finished doing a few rounds and working for an hour, my boss came up and told me there was a certain room that needed some special attention and that they were paying big and that the girls who usually does it, one was out sick and the other one quit.

"Alright. I'll do it. When do they get here?" I asked.

"Well, actually, in a few minutes. So if you can do me a favor and head towards the bar to grab some ice buckets and then take them to the room?" She asks.

"Sure." I reply.

I have never been into the VIP room before nor was I really interested in it. So when I walked in there it was really cool with mirrors all around, a few coffee tables where I was to put the buckets, along with LED lights around the couches and chairs. Then there was also a long table in the back for food and right as I headed out of the door, I went towards the bar to wait for the 'special' guests.

It wasn't too long before the front doors opened up and in walked a group of well dressed men. Maybe it's a bachelor party or something.

I walked up towards them and greeted them.

"Hi, I'm Vare and I'll be your server tonight." I greeted them with my smile.

They looked me up and down as most do, surprised that a curvy girl could possibly be here at a strip club.

"Alright Vare, take us to the room." He says.

As I turn around, him and his men begin following me back towards the room. Then after everybody takes a seat and gets situated, I begin taking the orders and head back towards the bar and kitchen.

Well, I guess this won't be so bad. Especially as I start remembering hearing about how big the tips are when you waitress the VIP room.

Next chapter will be posted soon! :)

CHAPTER 4: Now I Know

D ARIUS

Today was real busy and after finding her purse underneath my pillow where I had forgotten all about it until I rolled over in the morning and noticed it.

I'm not sure in why I even thought about returning it. In fact, I was going to have one of my guys go and do it but then after seeing what her address was on her license, I thought since it was along the way for me, I would drop it off.

In the end, I'm glad that I did. Although when I saw her this time, something was different. I personally began to feel something I had never felt before. It was a good feeling, nothing bad but at the same time it scared the hell out of me.

Before I returned her purse and before pulling up in front of her apartments, I started looking through her phone. Now the reason I do this is because I am cautious and paranoid as one is when you're in the line of work that I am in and I needed to make sure that she wasn't pretending to be afraid just to trick me into eventually getting my ass killed cause she's a diversion.

When I looked through her phone I could tell that she couldn't be with all these pictures of her and who I'm assuming is her sister or best friend. A smile creeps up on my face as I see she is just a normal girl.

Then we had pulled up and after going inside and pretending to use the restroom, I still had her phone in my pocket and don't know why I did it but I just put my number in her phone. Then went out and before saying anything, quietly placed it back into her purse on the counter while her back was turned to me.

I knew she was trying to reach for a knife but glad she hadn't. Then when my right hand guy, Terrano, came busting through the place like it's his, just to remind me about the meeting, I quickly snapped back into reality and left.

However, even on our way to the meeting, I wanted to hear her sweet voice again. But when I tried to call, I soon realized after not answering and trying a second time, that I had been blocked. I just got pissed off. NOBODY blocks me. NOBODY!

However, if that's how she wants to be then fine, fuck her then. I'm not gonna show a bit of interest then. She's nothing but another bitch anyways and just reminded me too in why I don't do relationships.

The moment we pulled up in front of the place we were having a meeting, I started feeling pumped with anger and irritation at the fact still she didn't answer. But I should thank her cause I needed to be this pumped up for this meeting.

After the meeting and a few more errands, I decided to check out my friends restaurant and grab a bite to eat. Then once I was finished I looked down at my phone and I saw a few texts from a buddy of mine who is gonna get married soon, which I tried talking him out of it but, he wants to still marry the slut who cheats on him and uses him all the time.

From the few pictures he has sent me too, I could tell he was having a good time but I honestly was real tired and the last thing I wanted was dirty girls grinding all over me. Besides, I know the owner to that club, I can go whenever. So I apologize and let him know I'll take him out later on cause I was too tired right now.

Then the moment I got home and plopped onto my bed face down while, I passed out.

*******************One week later

Today was the day I needed to collect the payments from all the people who pay me 'rent' we will say for me helping their businesses.

It was an all day job but I had nothing else to do today so I gave my usual guy I send to do it and told him I was gonna go instead.

It was good seeing that people were doing well. I hated to see good people struggle in trying to do what they love and what makes them happy without having the government screwing them over.

By night time, I decided there was one last place for me to go to and I wanted to get a drink anyways. So I hit up the strip club.

Once I walked in, I am always recognized and I say 'hi' to everybody as I make my way towards the bar where the owner, Bonnie, is at.

"Hey!" I greet her.

"Hey you! I wasn't expecting you." She says smiling.

This woman is like an older sister to me and she's bad ass also.

"Yeah I know. I decided to come and collect myself." I tell her.

"Well, come on, let's go to the office." She says and I follow after her.

After we sit down, she pours me a glass of Jack Daniels and hands me the glass before cheering me then we both shoot back the amount in there.

"I'd ask you how you're doing but from the looks of it, I can tell business is great." I chuckle.

"Yeah." She laughs too.

"Good." I reply as she unlocks the combination safe and then there's a knock at the door.

"Come in." She says as she digs through envelopes and documents for the money. The moment that door opened up, I saw her walk in......Variella.

"I finished cleaning up and counting my...." She says until she stops and looks at me wide-eyed.

"Oh good." Bonnie says. "I'll take the receipt and then you can head home sweetie." She says.

Neither me and Variella have stopped looking at each other with her still scared as hell and me trying to hide the amusement I have right now.

"Vare!" Bonnie says to get her attention and snaps Variella out of it.

"Uh, sorry. Here." She says before handing over the receipt.

"Thanks. I'll see you tomorrow." Bonnie tells her.

"Okay. Goodnight." Variella says without looking at me again.

"Oh and Vare? This is Mr. DeLucca. Mr. DeLucca, this is one of my best waitresses here." She introduces us.

"Nice to meet you Mr. DeLucca." Variella says as she holds out her hand to me.

To which I shake hers while gently circling my thumb around the top of her hand. I knew it affected her.

"Nice to meet you." I smirked at her.

She then jerked her hand from mine and nervously tucked a piece of hair behind her ear and said 'goodnight' again then turned around and left.

Well, at least now I know where she works.

Next Chapter will be posted soon! :)

CHAPTER 5: WTF?!?!

V ARIELLA

Fuck! Now he knows exactly where I work at. This is bad. He has both addresses.

I quickly grab my bag and jacket, say 'bye' to everyone before making my way outside in the back and tried starting the car. I tried starting it several times but it still wasn't turning on. So I tried calling the back of my towing membership card when I realized it had expired and I forgot I wasn't able to pay for that service anymore.

I placed my head on my hands that were holding the steering wheel and tried to calm myself down a little before thinking of what to do.

I couldn't afford a tow so I decided to call for an Uber or someone to come pick me up when I am startled by a knocking sound on my window.

I look and see it's Darius DeLucca. Seriously?!

I think about it at first if rather or not I want to or should roll down my window but seems like my hand had a mind of it's own because it rolled it down for me already.

"Need some help?" He asks.

"No thanks. I'm fine." I assure him.

"Well if it's fine then how come it wasn't starting?" He asks.

"I called for a tow truck. They'll be here in half an hour." I lie to him.

"Suuuuree..." He says sounding unconvinced.

"Don't you have someplace to be? Someone to torture or kill?!" I snapped at him annoyed and irritated by his presence. However, I immediately regretted what I just said as all I could see was an infuriated Darius, to say the least.

"You know what?! Fine! Sorry for trying to help your ass out." He snaps back at me while I knew I deserved that. At least he didn't shoot me or anything.

I rolled up my window after he walked towards his car a few spots down from mine and his driver opened the back passenger door then a moment later, took off.

I sat back in my chair letting out a breath I hadn't realized I was holding in. I need to learn to shut my mouth when it comes to people like him in particular.

****

It has now been several days since the last time I saw Darius and to be honest, at first, deep down inside I had wished I'd see him again but then quickly reminded myself what he does for a living and how it's better that I stay away from him.

Today I had a day off and decided to hang around at the apartment and order some take out while binge-watching between Hulu and Netflix.

It was a nice and relaxing day when I realized that I needed to also do some laundry. So I grabbed my detergent, softener and dryer sheets along with my hamper and began heading out to the laundry room downstairs.

When I showed up, a sixteen year old guy who I have known ever since I moved into my apartment a few years ago, greeted me with a 'what's up' nod.

He's got a buzzed head and reminds me of a Jared Leto.

"How are you doing tonight?" He asks me.

"Good, you?" I asked him.

"Good thanks." I reply.

"How's work going?" He smiles at me.

"It's good. I'm still not gonna get you in though." I smile back at him.

"Aww, damn." He says as he snaps his fingers while pretending he was disappointed.

After getting the washers going, I went to take a seat at one of the small round tables as I pulled out my phone and started playing some music since nobody was in here and I could dance if I wanted to even.

I purposely come in here this late at night in general because nobody is down here.

After my clothes were finished and I folded them up, I grabbed the basket of laundry and began heading back towards my place with earbuds now in my ears as I continued listening to music.

When I closed the door behind me I turned to set the basket down but ended up dropping it as I was startled all-of-a-sudden when I saw Darius sitting on my couch, sitting casually and grinning at me.

"How the hell did you get in here?!" I asked as I ripped the earbuds out of my ears, pissed.

"I have my ways." He smirks.

"Well you can get the hell out of here." I tell him as I point towards the door then bend down and pick up the basket of laundry to start heading towards my bedroom and as soon as I sat it down onto the bed, I turned around again and he was standing right there, startling me, ONCE again.

"We need to talk." He says.

"No we don't. Now get out of here before I..." I began to threaten but he cut me off and stepped closer to me.

"You'll what, call the cops?" He asks.

Now I felt real afraid and was quickly reminded in that moment that he of course wouldn't be afraid of the cops. So I began slowly backing up a little bit but was stopped as I hit my dresser.

"What are you doing here?" I asked.

He walks closer to me and leans in close enough to where he could kiss me.

"Like I said, we need to talk." He says as he looks down at my lips making me feel a bit more nervous.

"O-okay then. But lets go into the living room." I suggest.

A smile displays on his face before he turns and starts heading out after having me go in front of him. Which I'm sure it's so that he didn't risk me trying to hurt him with a blunt object or anything.

Once we got into the living room, he had me sit on the couch while he stood a few feet away while looking at me in a stance.

"Here's the deal. You know who I am and everything I'm capable of. I don't take 'no' for an answer and I sure as hell don't like being bothered." He says.

I try to hold in my laughter but clearly couldn't as he heard it and began scowling at me. Not to mention THAT was random. Why the hell would I care?!

"Sorry, but I find it odd that you're standing in MY apartment talking about how you don't like being bothered, yet that's what you're doing to me." I point out. Quite bravely I might add.

"Yes well, you are a bother." He states.

"And how is that?! You're the one breaking into my place, not to mention you keep somehow 'finding' me and interrupting my life. So what's your deal?" I asked rather irritated at this point.

"The deal is I'm not into relationships. I'm not the relationship kind." He says.

"Okay...And I care why? This Ransome shit is getting annoying. Can you get to the point already?!" I asked.

"Fine! I'm about to tell you something that involves you having to live with me." He mentions.

"Yeah, right." I try so hard to hold in my laughter at this point.

"I don't like it either but, your best friend, Morielle, asked me to do her this favor." He says.

"What are you talking about?" I asked confused.

"Of course." He says while looking down and shaking his head before looking back up at me to continue. "She didn't tell you."

"Tell me what?" I asked nervous and more scared than I have been before.

"She isn't REALLY a stripper. Her and I are cousins and she actually works for me. I've had her pose as a stripper because that's the one business I have helped where one of my old clients still goes to. I'm trying to collect a debt from him and she has been working there so that when he goes in, she can let me know. Then for some reason she became friends with you and because of that, you have been spotted." He finishes.

"Spotted?" I asked still confused and thinking this is his way of getting girls into sleeping with him.

"Yeah. So, anyways, you need to pack your things and come with me." He says while standing up.

"I'm not going anywhere with you and besides, how do I know you aren't just feeding me some bullshit?!" I asked while standing up with my arms crossed.

"Look, you can either do this the easy way or the hard way and trust me, the hard way you don't want. Now do as you're told." He says firmer.

"I said don't tell me what to do. And why don't you, once again, get the hell out of my apartment and leave me alone." I tell him before walking past him but was stopped as I felt him grab my arm and turn me to face him before pushing me against the wall with both my arms held down.

"Now you listen to me. Personally, I could give two shits about what happens to you, but for some reason, Morielle wants me to help you. So let's just do as we're told, alright?" He tells me.

With the look he is giving me right now along with the grip he has on my arms, I am terrified and feel as though I can't move.

"Fine." I finally agree.

He looks at me for a moment more and lets me go.

"Don't try anything funny." He says to me as I head into my bedroom to begin packing my things.

I can't go live with him. This has to be some kind of a cruel joke.

Wait, did I hear him correctly? Morielle is in the mafia?! WHAT THE FUCK?!!

Next chapter will be posted soon! :)

CHAPTER 6: Keep My Distance

D ARIUS

I was sitting in a meeting and just finished up with an important client of ours when I had gotten a call from my cousin, Morielle. She had told me that even though she didn't see the guy I was wanting her to look out for, she mentioned that she saw a couple of his men come in tonight which means their boss isn't too far away and will be showing his face real soon.

"Yeah well, we need to get Variella to a safe place. She has to stay at the house with us." She suggests.

"Fuck that! No! She doesn't know nor needs to know about our lifestyle. We can't trust her!" I exclaim. "Besides, this was why I told you not to make any friends or REAL ones." I remind her.

"Hey, I can't help it. Besides, if you don't do this, then when they realize that she's my best friend and has been seen with you, and you know they'll find out, would you rather have her blood on your hands or have them tell her?" She asks.

"Fuck! You owe me!" I reply after I think for a few moments before reply-
ing.

"Thank you!" She says sounding exhausted.

"Whatever." I roll my eyes. "Where is she now?" I ask.

"She's at her place. The sooner you do this, the better. So tonight would be
best. Just, don't be an asshole and don't freak her out. I will meet you guys
at the house and I will tell her everything." She says.

"Fine." I tell her and we hang up.

"Everything alright boss?" One of my men asks me.

"Yeah." I reply then we head to the car and I tell the driver to take me to her
apartment.

While on our way over, I begin thinking about having this girl stay with us
and hope that after Morielle tells her the truth, this girl doesn't go off and
blab it to people. That would put all of us at risk.

So after we arrived and I surprised her or I should say more like I startled
her, after our little argument and her tantrum/rant, she finally went into
her bedroom and packed several stuff.

She then grabbed her jacket and purse before we headed outside and down
the stairs. Once we got to the bottom, my driver grabbed all her bags and
opened the door for her to get in and then we took off a moment later.

I stayed on my phone mostly throughout the car ride home and while on
the ride over, I could hear her sniffling. Was she crying?

We finally pulled up to the house that I'm sure she won't ever forget from
that one night but hey, wasn't my fault she went out with an asshole. At
least I don't hide the fact I am one.

The moment I got out, I noticed she wasn't getting out. Infuriated, I balled my fists at my sides and began stomping around the front of the car towards her side until my right hand guy stopped me.

"Woah. Calm down." He says.

"Get out of my way." I warn him.

"Sir, I know it's not my place but you need to chill and see from her point of view. You just took from her place without an explanation and she has found out some things tonight. So relax." He tells me.

"I don't care. I'm not in the mood for this and am not gonna babysit her!" I tell him.

"Why don't you go inside and I'll take care of it." He says.

I think about it for a moment and decide that it would be better if he took care of it instead of me from the amount of anger I feel from not just this whole ordeal but also from the meeting earlier.

The moment I walked inside, I went into my office and locked the door then poured myself a few glasses of whiskey before sitting at my desk trying to think about everything.

I have so much frustration built up I need to let some go right now. So I take out my phone and dial up a girl I normally call every now and then when I need to relax.

Then right as I finish my third glass of whiskey, I hadn't realized how much time has gone by until I heard my sister come inside and by the time I got up and went out to greet her, she had ran up the stairs and into Variella's room which happened to be located a couple of rooms down from mine and Morielle's.

Soon after I see the front door open and in walks the girl I called.

"Hey sexy. It's been a while." She smiles.

"Yeah. Come on." I tell her as we head up to my bedroom and have some fun.

After she's finished, she leaves and I take a shower. Then I put some sweats on and start walking out to head down to the kitchen to grab something to eat.

It seems like everybody has passed out, except for of course the men outside protecting the house.

Then as soon as I turn the corner to walk into the kitchen, I stop when I notice that Variella has just finished making herself something to eat. She looks up and spots me and right away I can tell she had been crying as her eyes were red and puffy.

"I was just leaving." She says quietly and starts to walk out.

"Okay." I tell her not meaning to sound harsh but I guess it did because she stopped and turned towards me.

"Look, I know you don't want me here and I don't want to be here neither. But from what all I was told by Morielle, I know I don't have a choice. And I want you to also know that I promise I won't be in the way or try to cause you any trouble and I won't tell anyone about all this." She finishes and for some reason, maybe it's the way she sounded and the sadness in her voice that made me feel bad, but I did.

Though before I could say anything, she had already gone back upstairs.

Damn, maybe I had her all wrong. Plus, if Morielle says she's cool then I guess I should trust her.

I thought that by being an asshole that maybe she would ignore me and that way I don't have to worry about caring or getting too attached to her, but now, I'm confused as shit. Because I can't go through what I did again. I can't let THAT happen to someone like her.

Next chapter will be posted soon! :)

CHAPTER 7: Is That Fear?!?

V ARIELLA

It's been about a week now and I have done everything at all costs to avoid Darius just like he has been doing with me.

Today, since I had several more hours before my shift started, I decided to ask Kix to take me to the bookstore cause I have been looking for a new journal and have had some things I wanted to write down about what all has been going on.

Kix is one of Darius' right hand guys, aside from Terrano and is also the second driver who drives me and Morielle around so that we have protection always along with a couple of other guys. I swear it felt as though I was a celebrity or something.

Thankfully they don't go by what Darius tells them every time such as them keeping a distance from me and when I need their help, I will ask them. Luckily they like me or and have pity for me that they are willing to risk feeling Darius' wrath for defying his orders.

I was looking at all the journals when I felt somebody bump into me.

"I'm so sorry. I lost my balance there." The guy said.

He was about 5'8, had brown eyes and dark curly hair.

"It's okay." I smiled.

"Although to be honest, I'm glad it was a beautiful girl." He winks.

"Thanks." I chuckle.

"So, looking for a journal?" He asks.

"Yep." I replied.

"That's cool. I like the old leather bound ones myself." He says.

"Those are nice. But I'm actually looking for....ah! There it is." I say as I grab the same journal notebook I saw they had online.

"That is a nice one." He smiles.

"Well, hope you find one you like." I tell him before walking past him.

"Wait." He calls out.

"Yeah?" I stop and turn towards him.

"Would you like some coffee? I mean there's the coffee shop built in this place right behind you." He mentions.

"Uh, sure." I smiled and we headed towards the counter to pay for my journal and then he was nice enough to buy me a coffee.

We sat at a small rounded table near us and started talking.

Which I must have lost track of the time as I became fearful while he was talking about himself as soon as I looked up for a brief moment and saw a pissed off Darius stomp inside and start looking around the place until he spotted me.

"What's the matter?" The guy asks me with concern.

"Nothing. I've got to go." I tell him as I quickly grab my stuff and begin walking towards the door, passing Darius.

"Don't you walk away from me!" He says as he comes stomping after me.

"As far as I'm concerned, I can do whatever the hell I please!" I snap at him before Kix opens the door and I get into the car.

I was waiting for him to close the door but nope, Darius had to get in next to me. Then Kix got in and began taking off while I looked out the window avoiding Darius.

"Now you're gonna listen to me. You are NEVER and I mean NEVER going to pull that shit again on me. You don't call the shots around here and you are in NO position to be making friends or whatever that was with anyone. You got that?!" He asks.

I was furious but wanted to try and keep my cool.

"Did you hear me?!" He says more firmly and he grabs my arm.

I quickly remove it from his grasp and snap my head at him with a scowl.

"I got it!" I snapped at him then looked back out the window.

After finally pulling up to the house, I quickly got out and slammed the door before thanking Kix and heading inside the house.

"Oh hell no!" I heard Darius behind me as he closed his door. Then as soon as we got into the house, he grabbed me and turned me around to face him. "Don't be slamming doors and throwing a tantrum like a little child." He says.

"Me? Acting like a child? Please. You should take a look in the mirror." I snap back at him.

"Excuse me?" He asks.

"Yeah, you heard me! How dare you try and control me. You're not my father or somebody who gives two shits about me. So please stop acting like you do! And another thing, don't you ever try and pull that shit with me again! That guy was about to possibly ask me out!" I yell at him.

"Pff. I doubt it. That guy was too nervous he probably has never been on a date before or even has had sex." He says.

"Shut the fuck up! I'd rather him never been on a date before or even being a virgin for that matter than him being a man whore killer like yourself that uses blood money to take sluts out before tossing them away like they're nothing!" I say with a hint of regret and guilt but more of an 'I'm proud to stand up for myself.'

He looks taken back a bit along with everyone else that seemed to have been listening in on us. He quickly changes his look to being angry but I really don't want to hear or watch him throw a five year old tantrum.

So I turn on my heels and start walking towards my room to get prepared for work.

Maybe I had just dug my grave with him but he has no idea in how annoying and childish he's acting more than me.

I feared that things were going to only get worse from here on out. So I decided that I will TRY and big key word there is TRY, to play by these pathetic and stupid high school rules until I am able to leave.

I finish getting ready by putting my hair up in a high ponytail with curls at the end, hoop earrings, purple eye makeup and a skirt, along with fishnets, heels and tank.

While walking out, I pass the table where everybody is sitting at playing poker and laughing as they drink and smoke.

"Kix? Can I have you please take me to work?" I asked, completely ignoring Darius' glare.

"Of course." He smiles. "I'm out guys." He says while throwing in his cards and grabbing his keys.

"You're not going out like that!" Darius says. "It's a gentleman's club. Not a dirty strip club." He remarks.

"You're right. Then again, I didn't think this was a whorehouse." I smirk.

He scowled at me and I just smiled in satisfaction.

Kix and I started to head outside and he opened the front passenger door for me and then got in on his side and we started to take off. Though while pulling out the driveway, we noticed standing in the doorway leaning against the door frame was Darius, with his arms crossed as he continued scowling at the both of us.

"Damn, you're gonna get me into trouble." He says.

"Don't worry, he won't be nearly as upset with you as he is with me." I remark.

"True. But about that, you need to be careful. I mean, as hilarious and entertaining it is to all of us to see a woman talk back to him and him not hurting them, that's awesome, but also dangerous." He says.

Right then I swallowed a big painful lump in my throat that might have been created because of fear?!

Next chapter will be posted soon! :)

CHAPTER 8: What Am I Doing?!

D ARIUS

   She has some damn nerve talking to me like that. She's lucky she's Morielle's friend otherwise she'd be getting a rude awakening.

How DARE she disrespect me in MY house that I was nice enough to allow her to stay in.

Then to go dressing like she did? What the fuck?! She really pisses me off now to where I can't even focus on the game at hand. So I take back the last of my drink and grab my keys to head over towards one of my girls I normally sleep with more often then the one I brought here the other night.

I couldn't for some reason stop thinking about Variella and everything she said. Although I don't appreciate the attitude, she's right. I am an asshole and I what do I care if she goes out with a bitch ass punk?! A part of me was serious when I meant that she shouldn't because we can't allow someone to possibly ruin anything and try to bring any unnecessary attention to us not knowing who they know.

Then again, I'll admit that I did feel a little bit jealous. But I can't. I can't feel that way about her. If I get attached, people get hurt. I can't be responsible again for that.

Finally I make it to the girl's house and sit there in my car for a bit before going inside. Wait, why the fuck am I hesitating?! So I get out and make my way inside and she greets me the way I like her to by jumping into my arms while smashing her lips onto mine.

While kissing her, I tried real hard not to think of Variella but it was difficult. Then as soon as I carried the girl over towards the couch and lifted my head up to look at her, I saw Variella's face. Then that's when I stood up and got off of her.

"What's the matter?" She asks.

"I'm sorry but I can't do this." I tell her.

"Why?" She asks.

"I just can't." I tell her.

Fuck! Now she's got me apologizing which is something I NEVER do.

The moment I leave and get onto the road, I'm punching the steering wheel in frustration and for what? Some girl I barely know?! What the hell is wrong with me?!

When I make it back home, I assume everybody is asleep which it seems like they are, so I decide to head upstairs with a drink and lay in bed thinking.

I try looking for something to watch and end up watching a movie then come right back to boredom and end up eventually falling asleep.

****

After waking up the next morning, I headed downstairs and noticed that I wasn't the only one up but Kix was as he was making some stuff to eat. I haven't seen him cook in a while.

"Since when did you become Martha Stewart?" I teased him.

"Since my mother had me watch her when I was little. Don't be hatin'. You know you love my cooking." He says.

"Yeah. Can't argue with that." I chuckle a little to myself as I grabbed me a cup of coffee and sat down and noticed his knuckles were all red and bruised. "What's with your hand?" I ask.

"Got in a fight." He shrugs.

"Oh." I say brushing it off cause it's not any news. Probably somebody called him something they shouldn't have since he's gay and he kicked their ass, which he should because I have always done that to defend him. I mean, come on, he's gay, he's not a disease. Besides, they're born that way. Just like we are all born with the colors on our skin, they are born gay. I personally have never minded it.

"I'll make you some in a little while, but right now, this is for..." He says and stops as he looks up and smiles.

"Good morning." I hear her sweet voice.

"Good morning gorgeous." He smiles and winks at her. "It's almost ready." He says.

I notice as she turns from after pouring herself some milk that she has some of her hair covering the side of her face. I've seen many women have that look, including my mom. But wait, how did she.....

"What happened to your eye?" I asked while not looking at her and drinking more of my coffee.

I could feel both hers and Kix's surprised looks at me but ignored them.

"Nothing happened." She says.

"Here ya go." Kix chimes in and hands her the plate.

"Thanks." She smiles at him and then starts heading upstairs.

"So what happened?" I asked while looking at him.

"I took care of it." Kix says as he starts cracking some eggs to cook.

"Kix?! I know that look. My mother had the same look whenever my father would hit her. So one last time, what the hell happened?" I ask.

"It was just a couple of drunks. A few hours into her shift she was bothered by some guys and instead of saying anything about it, she just tried brushing it off. Then during her break, I noticed she went towards the restroom and I saw one of the guys follow her, so I followed him. I had gotten there just in time cause I could hear her muffled screams and the bathroom door was locked then as soon as I busted it open, I had noticed he had just punched her. So I took care of it." He finishes.

"Where the hell are the bouncers and security?" I asked.

"I don't know. Hitting on some girls probably. Although a couple of them were outside like they should be." He says.

I can't believe that. Some asshole tried to attack her.

"I'll have a talk with the manager." I tell him.

Next I get up and start to head upstairs to my room but stop as soon as I pass her room.

I debate in my head if rather or not I should go inside or not. I'm probably the LAST person she would want to see right now. So I stand there at her door for a moment before I close my eyes and take a deep breath in then let it out before I knock on the door.

What am I doing?!

Next chapter will be posted soon! :)

CHAPTER 9: What Have I Done THIS Time?!?

V ARIELLA

I appreciated everything that Kix did last night in defending me but I couldn't believe still he did that for me. Nobody has ever really fought for me before.

After I had finished eating the breakfast he made me, I walked into the bathroom to take a look at my eye and it wasn't too bad but still purplish blue.

I need to learn how to fight. Maybe I can have Kix teach me or something. However, I quickly get interrupted with my thoughts as I hear a knock at the door. Assuming it's Morielle just waking up or Kix, I answer it without thinking twice.

I was surprised to see it was Darius. I quickly try and hide my eye but it's too late, he has already seen it and he looks pissed off.

"Listen, if this is about last night and how I talked to you, I'm sorry. I know need to learn to keep my mouth shut." I tell him.

I had thought after saying that that he would walk away because that's why he was here.

"I deserved it." He says.

I am shocked. Did I just hear him correctly? Did he just apologize to me?

"Still." Was all I could say.

"What happened to your eye?" He asks.

"Nothing. I mean I'm sure Kix already told you." I tell him.

"Yeah but why didn't you tell the manager?" He asks.

"Because I have worked as a waitress at a restaurant before moving here and they took the customers word over mine because the owner thought I should be lucky for someone who looked like me to get that attention. Let alone, the fact those customers were his friends." Oh god why did I just tell him all of that?!?

"Well don't worry, it won't happen again." He says and before I could ask him what he meant he was already walking towards his bedroom.

I hope he doesn't do anything stupid.

Later on at night, after a couple hours into my shift, after talking with the manager and her apologizing to me for what happened, the rest of the time things seemed to be pretty laid back. Although she had nothing to be sorry about.

Then while walking over towards a table and serving some drinks, I looked up and noticed Darius was at the bar laughing with the bartender with a drink in his hand. Of course he was here and I bet I now knew what he meant by 'taking care of it.'

I walk up to the bar and have him turn to look at me.

"Why did you say anything?" I asked him.

"What are you talking about?" He asks.

"Don't play stupid with me. Why did you say anything? Now the manager and I'm sure everybody else thinks I'm a whining weak little bitch that can't defend herself or anything." I mention.

"Oh that." He pretends to now remember as to what I meant.

"Yes, THAT." I scowl.

"Calm down girl. A 'thank you' would be much better." He says with a smirk before taking a drink from his glass.

"I thought you didn't care?" I ask.

"Don't flatter yourself. I did it for the sake of the business." He says before finishing his drink and moving closer to my face.

"Yeah sure." I rolled my eyes. "You're such an asshole." I say under my breath and I guess he heard it because he grabbed my arm and pulled me even closer to him.

He looked like he was about to say something but something or should I say, someone caught his attention.

"If you'll excuse me, I've got something to do." He says while he looks over my shoulder behind me.

When I turn and see him walk away then see him kiss one of the best dancers on the cheek before she takes his hand and guides him back to a private room, I felt myself start to become upset. Some would probably call it jealousy but it couldn't be, right? There's no need to be jealous.

I continue on with my shift and forget everything that had just happened. Then at the end of my shift, I go into the restroom to make sure that my makeup hadn't ran and it hasn't, at least not enough to where my bruise showed.

Once I finished, I came walking out and since I was off work and Morielle had gotten off early, we decided to go out.

I normally am not a drinker and don't like to 'party party', I figured, it might be fun. So her and I got a ride from Kix.

The moment we walked in, Morielle had taken my hand and dragged me up towards the bar where she ordered us a couple of shots and then an actual drink before then taking me out onto the dance floor with her.

We danced for a while nonstop because the DJ was playing awesome songs. Then some guy asked Morielle to dance and she started grinding on him. Then I soon after felt two arms snake around my waist.

I turn around and notice this tall dark and handsome kind of a man, looking into my eyes, grinding on me.

We started dancing together and I felt like I was having the best time of my life.

I was feeling a little thirsty and we walked up to the bar and he bought me a drink. Then after taking a few sips, we started talking a little bit to get to know each other.

Then the DJ had put on one of my favorite songs so we headed back out onto the floor and started dancing together. I put my arms over his shoulders and he wrapped his arm around my waist, pulling me closer.

After a few moments of dancing, we looked at each other for a moment before leaning in closer towards me, but before our lips touched, I felt his hands being ripped off of me so fast that when I looked to see what was happening, I noticed Darius was beating him.

"Darius! Let him go!" I yelled out over the music and then tried pulling him off of the poor guy since he didn't hear me saying anything.

When he stops and turns to look at me, his hair is a little out of place and he's a little sweaty, not to mention furious. Then I feel him grab my hand tightly and start pulling me out, causing me a few times to almost trip and fall.

"Let me go!" I try yelling at him while trying to wriggle my hand free.

"Get in the car right now!" He says as he opens the front passenger door to his car.

"No." I tell him with my arms crossed.

"Variella, get in the fucking car now and don't make me tell you again!" He snaps at me.

A part of me doesn't want to but the other part of me reminds me that I don't want to piss him off. So I get in the car and he once he jumps into the drivers side, he starts taking off without putting on a seat belt.

I can't wait to see what I have done wrong this time!

Next chapter will be posted soon! :)I thought I would give you all another chapter today. ;)

CHAPTER 10: Why Why Why

D ARIUS

I had gone to the strip joint and spoke with the manager about some stuff and towards the end, mentioned about firing the security that didn't do their job with the situation of Variella getting hurt. She agreed and had felt bad. She already fired them and had two new ones coming in tomorrow for an interview. Then I headed out to the bar after we were done and talked to the bartender for a bit, having a drink and minding my own business when Variella comes up to me and starts complaining.

Luckily, since I wasn't in the mood to hear any bitching, I noticed behind her as I looked over shoulder there was a girl who happened to be a stripper and the manager's daughter that sometimes I would be given dances from in the past, however, she also happens to be dating someone that owes me money and had messaged me the other day to tell me she had my money for me. So I greeted her with a kiss on the cheek and decided to have her take me to a private room to hand me it so nobody knew what we were doing.

After I put the envelope of money in my pocket, she then sat down for a bit with me and we talked a little bit, well mostly she talked and brought up how she knows I like Variella and Variella likes me. Then after telling her a few things, she told me to stop using that as an excuse and get her before somebody else does.

As soon as we finished up and I came walking out, I noticed that Variella wasn't anywhere to be seen and when I went to the dressing room in the back, I saw that Morielle was also gone.

So I message Kix and he messages me back telling me where they're at and I immediately begin making my way over there.

I didn't expect to see Variella and some douche touching each other and the moment I saw him about to lean in to kiss her, I lost it and took the opportunity to yank him off and begin beating the shit out of him.

I was planning on stopping until I got a glimpse of his face and immediately recognized who he was and that he was an asshole who used to work for one of my enemies. He almost got me killed at one point, so yeah, I had a reason to be pissed off at him.

Once I feel her grab my arms though to try and get me to stop, I do when I see her horrified look on her face and then grab her hand then start pulling her towards the car out front and once she FINALLY got in, I took off to the house.

She immediately got out of the car before I was able to put it into park and then walked towards the front door and I had forgotten she had a key until she opened up the door and walked right in.

"I wanna talk to you!" I exclaim to her.

She continues walking up the stairs towards her room I'm assuming.

"Fuck you!" She says.

Damnit, why does she turn me on when she says that to me.

I start sprinting after her up the stairs and right as she tries closing the door, I grab it and walk right in then slam it shut behind me and start walking closer towards her until I'm close enough to grab her hand and spin her around to face me and push her up against the wall.

"Stop it." I tell her.

"No! Let go of me!" She says.

"I said stop it!" I exclaim more assertively as I hold both her wrists above her head.

"What the hell is your problem?!" She spits at me.

"You're my problem!" I blurt out.

"How am I your problem?! You're the one that won't leave me alone when I'm trying to keep my distance!" She snaps.

"I know and THAT'S the fucking problem!" I finally admit.

"What the hell are you talking about?" She says.

"Fuck!" I say exasperated and push myself off the wall and away from her.

"I can't fucking stay away from you. Believe me, I try to and it's for some damn reason, not working. My god, since the first night I caught you in my room, I couldn't get your face out of my head. Then to find out you work at one of the places I co-own and where my cousin works, not to mention living not that far from me. It's fucking hard." I confess. Pissed off at myself that I just exposed myself like that.

"You're so full of shit. Why are you doing this? Do you love trying to hurt others? Especially women? You get some fucking sick and twisted pleasure fucking with emotions that way? You can't just get jealous and then act like you care one moment when you're sleeping with other women! I'm not a menu item, you can't just order me whenever the hell you like to." She says.

"I know you're not. Shit, I'm putting everything out on the table for you and yet you're gonna just take it and throw it away. It's no wonder you're single." I remark but didn't mean that to come out.

I can see the pain and hurt in her eyes.

"Go to hell. I have chosen to be single because I'm tired of doing EVERY-THING in the relationship and changing my appearance and who I am to fit your 'guy' needs only in the end to be treated like shit and be unappreciated and unwanted. And I am so fucking sick of it." She says as she fights back tears.

Wow, now I feel like a bigger douche bag than before. Oh my god, I always swore I would never turn into my father but look at me now, I am. I'm so afraid of repeating the past with my ex that, I let it show through anger.

"Variella..." I start to say.

"Now, please leave." She says.

Then walks past me towards the door and before she has the chance to open it up, I hold closed the door.

"Wait." I say with my mouth so close to her ear and the scent from her amazing perfume drives me crazy as it invades my nostrils and I want so badly to kiss her right now.

"Don't do this." I hear her say through sniffles.

I turn her around and she looks at me with tears falling down her face already. She then switches from looking sad to being real upset and starts pushing me away.

"What the hell is the matter with you?!" She says and then comes up to me again, pushing me back again and then again until I grab her wrists to stop her without squeezing too tightly then push her back onto her bed with her wrists again held down above her head while on top of her.

We look into each other's eyes for a moment before I begin to say anything and can start to notice the bruise on her eye a little bit.

"I'm sorry." Was all I could say as all I could see was what my father did to my mom when she fought back and he hit her harder making her cry. I know I didn't give her the black eye but feels like I did.

I then get up and start to leave but before I do, I turn a little and tell her one last thing.

"You have every right to hate me. I'm sorry for everything I've said and done to you. It's not right and......and I'm sorry." I tell her while choking back on some tears before opening the door and leaving to head to my room.

Why am I such a fuck up?! Why why why?

Next chapter will be posted soon! :)

CHAPTER 11: Please Let This Work

V ARIELLA

It has been a week now since I last seen and talked with Darius in my bedroom that night.

I don't know why but I was missing him. Kix told me he was on a trip for business with his other right hand guy that he can trust, Terrano and would be back soon. However, before he came back, I had thought I would get opinions from Morielle and Kix. Although Morielle said there were some things she didn't want to because she felt it was better to hear it from him.

So then I sat with Kix watching TV before I asked him anything.

"Kix?" I ask.

"Yeah?" He replies.

"You've known Darius a long time, right?" I ask him.

"Of course." He says before shoveling popcorn in his mouth.

"What can you tell me about him?" I ask and I feel as though I asked him something that seemed to have been not so much a shock but it seemed to have been serious since he shut off the TV and set down his popcorn.

"Well, for starters, something you need to know about him is that he isn't really an asshole. I mean, it's hard to see that but, only a few see that side of him anyways. He'll kill me for telling you all of this but, I can tell you both like each other and to be honest, I think you're both great for each other even. Though if you really want to try and get to know him, which I think you should, there's some things you need to know." He begins.

"Like what?" I ask.

"For one thing, he didn't necessarily choose this life. It was kind of chosen for him. He grew up as the son of one of the most fearful boss' of the mafia. He tried hard to escape from the name and the lifestyle but, his father always found a way to pull him back in. And as crazy as it sounds, he actually did it for his mom." He says.

"What do you mean?" I ask curious and yet confused.

"His father knew how much Darius loved his mother and always was seeking approval from his father. So his father threatened him. He promised Darius that he would stop cheating and hitting his mother if he would work for him. So he did. Because Darius knew he couldn't fight his father. Well, although later on, Darius did learn how to fight really good. But one day, he finds out that his mother was pregnant and when she was almost two months along, he saw his father beat on her until she was dead. He literally beat her to death and killed the baby." Kix says with tears.

"Oh my god." I say under my breath.

"That was the first night Darius killed anyone. He shot his father after his dad chased him out of the room and into his dad's office and grabbed the gun in the drawer and didn't hesitate to pull the trigger." He finishes.

"Wow." I say. "So, after he did that, the authorities didn't take him away?" I ask.

"Nope." He says popping the 'p'. "His father owned a lot of people including the big guys. Another reason he stayed, was because he has been trying to stop trafficking. Trying to make deals with guys that run that kind of shit and then hand evidence over to the FBI and CIA. The only people he hurts, are criminals that have done far worse than him. Some of them have been women. That's the only time he has ever hurt a woman." He tells me.

"Oh." I say feeling horrible.

"Now, granted he has been a bit of a man whore throughout the years but has never forced anyone. And I think what's really hard for him is you remind him of his girlfriend from years ago."

"What do you mean?"

"One night we were doing a job and something went wrong as things do sometimes and she was raped and killed by a gang. Right in front of his eyes. Which is why it's hard for him to get close to anybody, even if he wants to." He says the last part looking at me.

"I see. I feel so bad from what all I said to him the night before he left. The night we had that fight, I could hear the genuine and sincerity in his tone of voice when he apologized. I should have told him that night or at least the next day before he left on his trip that I was sorry. He was right, there is a reason nobody wants me."

"I know somebody that does." He smiles at me as I return the smile.

"Well, he comes back tomorrow so, I guess I can try and think of something to try and make him talk to me and allow me to apologize."

"Well, there might be one way. Tomorrow is his birthday. He hardly likes to celebrate it but if we do a surprise party, he will have no choice BUT to have fun and also let loose enough for you to be able to talk to him." He winks at me.

"Okay." I smile. "Let's plan one."

"Alright. How about I let everyone know and you and Morielle go ahead and get the decor, food and everything you need, then we'll throw one."

"Cool." I smile.

We both get up and begin to do what we each were going to and I ran upstairs, well actually, I don't run, but I quickly got up the stairs and caught my breath a little before waking her up.

She was screaming with excitement and had told me that she has been dying to throw a party for the longest time and since we had a pool in the back along with a grill area and it was gonna be hotter than satan's balls this weekend, we decided to make it a pool party and take the weekend off from work.

I hope he likes all of this and Kix was right. Because if he's upset about this then I give up.

Next chapter will be posted soon! :)

That's right guys, I thought of giving you two chapters from this story today. :):) Enjoy! :):):)

CHAPTER 12: Go Out With Me

D ARIUS

I was livid. This fucker is such a sick fuck that instead of turning him over to the authorities, I decided to take matters into my own hands.

Terrano, one of my right hand guys who travels with me mostly, other than Kix whom I left to stay at home to watch the girls, has this guy all tied up, naked, in a chair.

He was covered head to toe in blood and bruises, wounds that will never heal as he still remained the way he's always been, an asshole.

"So you enjoy raping women and selling their daughters to old disgusting perverts like yourself?" I ask with my head cocked to the side and such venom.

"If you think this little charade is gonna make me say sorry or beg you to stop, you're wrong." He says with an evil chuckle and spits out blood.

"I know you aren't gonna change your mind and apologize. Because you're a sick and twisted bastard. I just wanted to see how much you bled. Now for my last trick of the night." I smirk at him in an evil way before I have Terrano grab the hot cast iron made pliers that was just being removed from the fire we had it over to get it nice and hot, I had him hand it to me after I put a thick glove on. I looked at it for a moment and then walked up towards him, clamped it down onto his small penis, hearing the sizzling sound of his flesh burning from the heat before I then yank it off to let him bleed out.

"Ah fuck, boss!" Terrano says over the man's screams as he grabs himself in pain.

"Terrano, have the guys clean this up. I have a flight to catch in a couple of hours and need to take a shower." I tell him while dropping the clamps before leaving.

Some of my guys that watched the whole thing were gagging and holding themselves as I just left.

I stood under the water in the shower for a while before starting to clean myself and I started to tear up as I thought about my ex girlfriend and how she was gang raped after being kidnapped then sold by her own father. I should have protected her. But I failed her instead.

Once I was finished with my shower and got dressed, I started heading to the airport to head back home.

It wasn't until I had gotten on the plane that I had realized it was even my birthday. Which I don't do anything special for it. I don't deserve it for everything I have done.

I try to get it out of my head and sleep the whole plane ride back and so that I don't have to think about Variella. My god how she reminds me of my ex girlfriend.

She has the same effect on me only, Variella has a pull on me stronger than my ex ever did, but she makes me feel calm and comforted. She's beautiful inside and out and has curves that drive me crazy as hell.

****

Finally the plane lands and I feel real rested. So maybe tonight I'll go out and have some fun.

Once I get home though and open the door to walk in, I set down my bag of stuff and then am startled as people pop out of nowhere all yelling at the same time, "Happy Birthday!"

"What the fuck?!" I asked confused.

"Hey man, happy birthday!" Terrano says as he hits my shoulder and smiles.

"What the hell?! Why did you do all this?" I asked.

"It wasn't our idea." Kix says.

"It was mine." I hear Variella say as she comes walking out with a small smile.

I was surprised and shocked but also, moved a little? I couldn't help but smile a little as a 'thank you' to her.

Throughout the party, I couldn't help but feel relaxed and able to have fun as we all were hanging out in our swimsuits as we ate some good barbecue that Kix grilled, swam and had the most fun I had in a long time.

While some people left after we hung out around the bonfire pit I had in the backyard, others stayed there while I noticed Variella getting up to head inside so she could wash her hands under the faucet in the kitchen sink from the messy s'mores we all just had.

When I got inside, I closed the sliding glass door behind me and walked up behind her and kept a close distance between us.

"Thank you." I tell her and I guess I accidentally startled her by saying that.

"Oh my god." She gasps.

"Sorry. I didn't mean to scare you." I tell her.

"It's okay." She says. "Happy birthday." She smiles.

"Thanks." I smile back at her.

We both share a moment of silence before saying anything.

"Well, I'm gonna head to bed. I'll see you in the morning." She says.

She might have told me that but her body language was throwing me through a loop as it was saying 'take me.' I could tell by the way she bit her lower lip a little.

So I followed behind her without her knowing and as soon as she went into her room, I closed the door behind me and she turned around and was surprised to see me in here but at the same time, I could tell she was also happy.

I don't even say anything as I walk right up towards her and grab her face then smash my lips onto hers and we began making out.

I then pushed her up against the wall only this time was for a good reason and I felt her hands on the sides of my face and kissed me back, allowing my tongue to enter her mouth.

When we stopped for a moment to catch our breaths and looked into each other's eyes.

"I'm sorry. I'm sorry for everything and I'm sorry for just kissing you like I just did I just couldn't help it. I have wanted you for so long and I just couldn't hold it in anymore." I confess.

"I've wanted the same thing." She tells me.

"Be mine. Go on a date with me." I ask as I slowly move my mouth and place kisses on the side of her neck.

"Okay." She moans.

"Mmm.." I moan and next grab her thighs and wrap her legs around my waist as she wraps her arms over my shoulders and mine on her ass as I carry her over towards the bed while laying on top of her and kissing her from her mouth to her neck.

To be continued......

Next chapter will be posted soon! :)

CHAPTER 13: Happy Birthday

V ARIELLA

It didn't register until he was kissing me on the side of my neck while he was on top of me in the bed that I had just agreed to go out on a date with him and be his girl?

I thought he hated me though? Meanwhile, I can't even think about that right now or anything else for that matter, even the people downstairs still because of how amazing his lips feel against my skin along with his hands gripping onto one of my breasts on the outside of my shirt.

"Mmmm." I moan.

"I want you so bad." He says.

"I want you too." I tell him.

He then sits me up and we both remove our shirts and then I start pulling down his board shorts as he hurries and kicks them off to where now he's fully naked and I am speechless. I mean, I already have gotten a good look at his physique earlier but naked, wow. Not to mention his size.

I begin stroking his cock as we go back to kissing until he starts removing my shorts and panties then tossing them onto the floor before I remove my bra and do the same thing.

He looks at my body and I start to cover my chest because I'm not sure in what he's thinking right now.

"You are so beautiful." He tells me while looking into my eyes. "Don't ever cover yourself around me." He tells me.

I smile and then turn him onto his back and straddle his waist with my legs.

"It's your birthday." I tell him.

I then bend back down to continue kissing him before kissing down to his neck, to his chest then his stomach. Making it all the way down to his long hard shaft.

I start stroking it with my hand up and down slowly at first and then use my mouth by putting the tip at first in then moving my mouth down further, taking him inch by inch then eventually speeding it up and stroking his cock using both my mouth and hand.

"Fuck..." He moans as he grips onto my hair.

I begin moaning also as I start moving my head up and down faster and faster until I feel him pull my hair back enough to have me stop and look up at him.

He then sits up, grabs my chin and lifts it up as he smashes his lips onto mine before pushing me onto my back again and starts moving his mouth hungrily down my neck then between the valley of my breasts and then takes one nipple into his mouth, making me arch my back a little in pleasure.

His tongue moves over each nipple while his hand kneads the other one before giving the same attention to the other one.

His lips start to move all the way down to in between my legs and right away I feel his tongue move slowly up and down between my folds a few times, teasing me, driving me crazy before flicking at my sweet bud starting off slow and then going faster more and more.

I buck my hips up and down a little from the pleasure while he holds down my legs and then slides in one finger at first then two fingers and instantly starts thrusting them in and out faster and faster while continuing to flick at my clit with his tongue until I finally reach my high and come.

"Oh. My. God." I say breathlessly. "Nobody has ever given me an orgasm before." I tell him.

"Mm...Glad I'm the first, but I'm not done yet." He tells me.

The next thing I see is him pulling a condom from his pants and tearing open the condom wrapper, then rolls it on and before I can say anything, I feel him thrust deep inside of me hard.

While smashing his lips onto mine, he starts off thrusting at a steady pace and then begins picking it up going faster and harder.

"Mmm...ahh..." I start to moan while gripping onto his sides.

He starts burying his face into the crook of my neck, kissing me while continuing bringing me more and more pleasure.

"You're so tight baby. You feel so good." He grunts as he picks up the pace.

"Mmm...so do you." I moan. "Shit, you're gonna make me come again." I moan to him.

"Come all over me. I want to feel and hear you coming on my cock baby." He says in my ear.

That right there sends me off quickly into a high making me climax more and more. Then as soon as I feel him continuing to thrust inside of me while he rubs my clit at the same time until finally I reach my climax and moan out loud while coming all over his cock.

Not too long after that, he too comes in the condom while thrusting one last time and moaning himself before then collapsing on top of me breathless.

"Fuck that was amazing." He tells me.

"Yes it was." I giggle.

Then he lifts himself up and pulls out then tosses the condom into the trash can before he lays on his back and pulls me close.

"You are amazing." He says. "This was the best birthday ever."

"I'm glad. But did you really mean what you said about how you feel about me and that you wanted to take me out?"

I don't know why I asked. I started to regret saying it as I heard him sigh real big.

"I meant every word. You had me hooked since the moment I first met you. I've just been afraid, believe it or not." He says.

The thing about him saying that is I know why and what he's talking about.

Next chapter will be posted soon! :)

I thought once again, I would do 2 chapters for this story today for you guys. Enjoy. :):)

CHAPTER 14: Don't Try To Change Me

D ARIUS

It was a great birthday yesterday and I finally gave in and asked Variella out.

When I woke up this morning, I had noticed she wasn't next to me and I started heading downstairs after putting some pants on and saw she was making some breakfast.

She looked so hot. Her curves drive me crazy and all I can think of now is how great it is that she is all mine and nobody else's.

I wall into the kitchen while her back is towards me and wrap my arms around her waist as I kiss the side of her neck.

"Good morning." I tell her.

"Morning." She replies as she turns and gives me a kiss on the cheek.

"It smells great." I tell her as I give her a peck on the cheek before I head over towards the coffeemaker to pour me some coffee.

"It should taste great too." She replies.

"I'm starving." I tell her while sitting down at the breakfast nook on a bar stool as she comes walking over with two plates and we start eating together.

"So what's the plan for today?" She asks me.

"Well, I need to meet with somebody and then afterwards, when I came back tonight, I was thinking of taking you out." I wink at her.

"Okay." She smiles.

After we finished with breakfast, we both headed upstairs to take a shower and everyone had seemed to be still sleeping. Which was fine by us because we decided to have some shower sex.

Then afterwards, she gave me a kiss goodbye before me and my guys headed over to the meeting and I have to admit, I can get used to this.

It's amazing how you convince yourself for so long that you don't deserve love. Yet then when there's someone like Variella who comes into your life that easily could have turned me down and say 'no' to me and what I do, instead gives me a chance. Is willing to see past what I do.

I start to get myself ready however for the meeting and throughout the entire time, I couldn't concentrate like normal without thinking about her. Man, already she has got me hooked.

When the meeting was finally over, I had Terrano drive us towards a few more runs before heading back home and for most of the time, I was texting Variella and make sure she was ready tonight.

I already had her have the day off after talking to the boss there and I couldn't wait to see what she was wearing.

When we got back to the house, I quickly headed upstairs after hearing that Variella was almost done getting ready.

Once I finished I headed downstairs and she was already there talking with Kix while wearing a nice laced dress that showed off her sexy ass curves, along with black tights and a pair of heels. I could feel my cock start to twitch in my pants.

"Hey man." Kix says.

"Hey." I reply.

She stands up and looks at me.

"Ready to go?" She asks with a smile.

"Yeah. But damn, you look amazing and hot as hell right now." I comment while I eye her up and down.

"Thanks." She blushes. "You look hot also."

"I know." I joke.

We head to the car and start to make our way towards the restaurant. After arriving, we walk hand-in-hand inside and give our order.

"I'm glad you asked me out." She smiles at me.

"Me too." I tell her while rubbing my thumb gently over her hand.

"You know..." She begins but is interrupted from the waiter bringing our order.

Which honestly, I didn't like very much. I know it's not his fault but the asshole got on my bad side the moment he looked at Variella with disgust. I had tried to ignore it but then he said something under his breath that made me lose it.

"Here you are sir. And here you are miss. Disgusting pig." He says the last part under his breath.

"That's it." I say while standing up and punching him so hard he falls back onto the empty table behind him.

"Don't you EVER disrespect anybody like that again, especially my girl." I tell him before bending over him and pulling him up by his collar to continue beating his face up.

Then I feel myself getting yanked off by a few waiters and notice the manager quickly come running out.

"Mr. DeLucca. What the hell is going on?" He asks.

"This low-life prick, disrespected my girl and I was just teaching him a lesson." I explain.

The manager and I go way back and have known each other for years.

"I'm so sorry Mr. DeLucca, I'll take care of this right away." He says and grabs the waiter by the collar to pick him up and starts pulling him towards the back while I turn and look back at Variella who I notice is gone.

I start heading outside to look for her and see her standing in front of the restaurant looking upset while trying to hold herself to keep herself warm.

"Hey, why did you leave?" I ask.

"Because what you did in there, as great as it was of you defending me, it was also embarassing. I mean everyone was looking at us and not to mention, you just punched the guy repeatedly as if you wanted to kill him. Do you always resort to that?" She asks with tears rimming around her eyes.

"Variella, this is who I am. Somebody disrespects me, my family or anybody else I car about, I'm defend them and teach them a lesson. That's who I am." I explain.

"So if I got you upset or disrespected you, you would do the same thing to me?" She asks.

"Of course not. Baby look at me." I tell her as I walk closer to her and lift her chin up to look at me. "Look I'm sorry if I scared and embarrassed you. I'll try and work on that okay?"

"I'm sorry but, it's just, I hate being around someone who resorts to violence like that. I mean it looked like you wanted to kill him and I know you are this big mafia boss man but, if you want to be with me, you can't do things like that." She says as tears fall down her face.

I look at her for a moment more and then start seeing in her eyes just how much fear I have just made her feel.

"I promise I will work on it. I don't want to screw this up." I assure her.

She then nods and as I wipe away a few tears, I lean in and give her a passionate kiss.

So instead of having dinner at the restaurant, since I ruined it, I had her choose what she wanted. Then we drove to a place that had a great view of the night sky and watching the moonlight bounce off the bay water while we sat on a blanket.

This girl is changing me and even though I'm not really complaining, I can't help but fear as to what she's doing to me. I hope she doesn't try and change me entirely.

Next chapter will be posted soon! :)

Hey guys, sorry it's been a couple of days since I posted for this and the other story, I have been real busy with work. But I'm again, back on track again. So here's this one and will have a chapter posted for the other one too in a moment. :):) Love you all. :)

CHAPTER 15: Become More Understanding

V ARIELLA

It's been already almost two weeks since I've started dating Darius and things have been going really good. He seems to be getting better at controlling his temper more.

That night a couple weeks ago when he lost his cool on our first date, I couldn't help but get scared because that's what Blake used to be like.

Tonight, I was asked to cover one of the other cocktail waitresses shift so I had to do a double shift practically which was okay since I needed the money.

Darius still doesn't like that I want to still work and not have him take care of me. I mean, I know it makes him feel better and I do let him for the most part, pay for what he wants to for me but otherwise, I actually enjoy making my own money and paying for things.

Tonight was real busy at the gentleman's club but that just meant the tips were great. While I was on break, I had gotten a text from Darius saying how much he missed me and that he was gonna stop by a little before my shift ended and then take us home.

This guy really does know how to make me smile and feel all giddy inside. So I message him back and once my break is over, I head back to making my rounds.

Then while dropping an order off at the bar, I heard a voice that made me feel sick and scared.

"Well look who I've found." He says.

I try and remember that I'm at work and to not make a scene of any kind. Besides, Darius will be here soon, so I treat him like any other customer.

"Hi Blake." I tell him.

"I didn't know that allowed people your size to work here. Must have sucked the boss' dick. You were always good at that." He smirks as he takes a drink from his glass of brandy.

"Whatever Blake." I roll my eyes.

Luckily the bartender sets the drinks on my tray and as I pick it up and start to walk off, I feel him grab my arm causing me to drop the tray causing the glasses to break all over the floor.

"Let go of me." I tell him as I try breaking free from his grasp.

"You're sleeping with that Darius guy aren't you?! Aren't you you fucking slut?!" He says right before slapping me hard across the face.

"Hey! Hey! Hey!" I hear the bartender yell and hop over the counter but before the bartender could get a hold of him, I noticed Darius behind Blake, turn him around to face him and threw a hard punch at Blake who then of course threw a punch at him causing them to break out into a brawl.

It didn't last too long after I saw the manager and several of her new security guards come and break it up. Darius then grabbed my hand and we started to leave.

Once we got into the car and headed home, throughout the entire ride, he just white knuckled the steering wheel while keeping silent.

I almost felt like I was in trouble. I hope he doesn't think that I asked him to go or anything.

When we pulled up, he still had the pissed off look and I noticed his knuckles were all bruised and bloodied a little bit. I wanted to suggest to clean them up but couldn't.

Throughout the entire time from when we got out of the car, walked inside the house and him getting a drink, we said nothing to each other.

"Look, I..." I started but he cut me off.

"You're quitting that job and staying here." He says while looking down at his glass.

"What? I'm not doing that." I tell him.

Here we go again.

"Yes you are." He says as he glares at me before taking a drink and setting down his glass.

"No, I'm not. We talked about this." I try and remind him but he doesn't want to hear any of it.

"You're gonna do as I tell you, Variella. You don't understand what Blake is capable of." He says.

"Oh I don't? Remember the first night you and I met and you found out what I was doing there?" I asked glaring back at him.

"Oh big deal. He brought you to a fucking orgy. He does far worse things than that." He says. "But just like before though, you think of this all as some sort of a game." He tells me.

"I'm not doing this right now with you. You can be so fucking exhausting." I say under my breath while leaving and heading upstairs.

The right side of my face really hurts from where Blake slapped me at and I start to try and get ready for bed when I hear the door shut roughly.

"Now let me explain to you the severity of why I care so much." He says in an assertive tone but yet, calming at the same time. "This asshole is partners with one of the biggest gang leaders out there that also runs a trafficking business." He tells me. "But that's not all." He says as he walks towards the bed and lets out a breath before continuing.

"A few years ago, him and I had a falling out that resulted in me almost getting killed. He tried to frame me for something he stole. Since then we have been enemies. You have to understand Variella, I am protective because I know what all can happen just with you being with me. Then to have to worry about him and something happening to you I just, I won't be able to live with myself. I lost someone years ago that I loved. Then Blake and that asshole kidnapped her and sold her to someone. I spent almost a year looking for her and finally found her. But she was dead. She had been raped and beaten." He confesses through frustration with his face in his hands.

So I sit down next to him and take his hand in mine as I enlace our fingers. He looks at me.

"I'm sorry. I'll try and be more understanding. I guess since you're trying to control your anger more, I could at least do this." I tell him.

He looks me in the eyes and holds the side of my face before leaning in and giving me a kiss.

Next chapter will be posted soon! :)

CHAPTER 16: Somebody Needs Reminding

D ARIUS

I'm glad that she does understand what all is going on. It makes things a lot easier.

"So boss, what do you think we should do about Blake and his crew?" One of my guys ask.

"For now we'll just keep on the lookout for anything that might ruin us." I tell them.

"And what about Variella?" He asks.

"What about her?" I asked.

"Well, she used to date Blake and we heard he ran into her the other night at the club." He mentions.

"And I took care of it. Don't worry, she understands the measures I am having to take and that she will need to try and do. So there won't be an issue." I say.

"Alright...." The guy says in a way that sounded as though he doesn't trust her or something.

"What was that? Are you questioning my girl?" I glared at him.

"No Sir, just that you haven't known her for very long." He says.

"I think we're done here. The meetings over." I say and stand while not taking my eyes off of him.

Everyone gets up and we start to all head out to our cars and while on the way back, I couldn't stop thinking about what that guy said. I can't believe he had the nerve to question about trusting Variella. I mean sure it's true that I barely know her but I trust her.

When I got back home, I was expecting to be greeted with a hug and a kiss or at least seeing Variella but she was nowhere to be seen.

I then walked over towards Kix and asked him where she was.

"Oh, she's outside in the pool. She seemed kind of down." He says.

I feel bad as I'm sure some of it if not all of it is because of me. So I quickly head upstairs and get into my swim trunks and head downstairs and see she's hanging in the deep end with her arms on the outside of the pool as she moves her feet around a little.

Dive into the water and begin swimming all the way up to her and grab her sides as I come up for air, combing my hair back with my hand. Before wrapping her arms around my shoulders as I wrap mine around her waist and start kissing her.

I hear that sexy and adorable giggle that she does.

"I missed you today." She tells me.

"I missed you too." I tell her. "Kix just told me you were feeling down."

"A little." She admits.

"But why." I asked.

"Well, I got a call from the club saying that I was let go."

"Ohhh." I say as I realize I forgot to tell her that it was because of me.

"What?" She asks.

"Don't get upset but, I had her let you go." I tell her.

"What? Why the hell did you do that?" She punches my chest while trying to push me away.

"Because I had to and besides, you said that you were willing to do whatever it took to keep you safe and well, that's it. You can't work or any of that with Blake and others getting the chance to getting to you." I try and remind her.

"I wish you would have told me still. I mean, if I can't work then what? You want me to stay and do what exactly? I've supported myself for as long as I can remember. Never took handouts or had anyone really support me. I don't know if I can do that." She tells me and lets me go before swimming past me.

I stop her by grabbing her ankles and she goes under water real fast then comes back up as I start pulling her towards me.

"Do I need to remind you about why we're doing this?" I ask her in between the kisses I place gently onto her neck.

"No." I hear her say while licking her lips and moaning.

"I think I do." I say in her ear while gripping her ass before smashing my lips onto hers.

We get out of the pool and go up towards the bedroom where I teach her a very good lesson. That from the amount of orgasms I gave her and how sore I made her, she might remember.

Next chapter will be posted soon! :)

CHAPTER 17: Do As I say! Please!

V ARIELLA

Morielle was forced to quit the club also not too long after me because he felt it was getting too dangerous for herself, plus not to mention the fact that I already have my men watching him and his crew so that if he tried anything, Darius would know all about it before it happened.

I did feel more safe than I think I ever have ever in my life. Although, it has been getting some use to for me to be okay with this whole not making my own money thing.

Today I was sitting with Morielle watching a movie and during the middle of the movie, she randomly paused it.

"I have to tell you something." She says.

"What?" I asked feeling a bit nervous.

"You can't tell anyone, especially Darius." She begins.

"Okay. Are you pregnant or something?" I joke.

"No. But I am going out with Torrence." She says.

"Really?! Oh my god you guys are perfect together! But why not tell Darius?" I asked.

"He's like a protective older brother. It wouldn't be pretty. I mean, we want to tell him but not yet." She tells me.

"Okay. I promise that I won't say anything but I am really happy for you both." I smile and hug her.

"Thanks." She smiles. "I just had to tell somebody."

"Well I'm happy to be the one you told." I tell her.

We both begin to laugh and then get up to get ready for when the guys come and pick us up to take us out to dinner.

The guys of course were a little late but whatever, cause I was way too hungry to care about starting anything. So we just got into the car and we headed on off to the restaurant.

Once we arrived and were seated, I could tell that Torrence and Morielle were both dying to kiss and I already knee they were holding each other's hands underneath the table as I had noticed it when I accidentally dropped my napkin onto the floor and bent over to pick it up.

It's a shame though that they have to keep it a secret from Darius. At least for now.

After the waiter brought us our food, we continued laughing, talking, drinking some wine and having a real great time.

Then as it got later, we decided to all call it a night when we headed outside towards the car and were stopped by some shady ass guys that I didn't get a good feeling from. Though it seemed that Darius knew them.

"Well look who we have here." The asshole said.

"Larry." I hear Darius greet him.

"It's been a long time." Larry tells Darius with a smirk.

"Not long enough." Darius says as I start to feel his grip on my hand start to get tighter.

"Ow." I say under my breath.

"Is this your new play toy?" The guy says as he looks me up and down.

Darius next tells me and Morielle to get into the car. I wanted to say no but I didn't want him to become more angry and snap at me, so I did as I was told.

We both got into the car while him and Torrence both stayed outside.

Now, because Darius has bullet proof glass on his car windows, all we could hear were muffles.

"I wonder what they're saying out there." I say more to myself.

"Whatever it is, I know it's not good. That guy is crazier than Blake to be honest." Morielle tells me.

"What do you mean?" I asked her.

Next I hear them getting louder and notice Larry throw a punch at Darius who ducked from it and then came back swinging with Torrence doing the same as they both were kicking the guys' asses.

Then finally, it ended and Darius along with Torrence hurried and got into the car then Torrence sped off back towards the house.

"FUCK!! FUCK! FUCK!" Darius begins punching the back of the front passenger seat.

"Calm down baby. Who was that?" I ask.

"I'll tell you later. But for now, as soon as we get home, we are packing our shit and leaving for a while." He tells me.

"What? But..." I started and he stopped me.

"Please, just do as I tell you to. I'll explain everything later." He says trying not to snap at me but it was too late as I had already felt that's what he just did.

Next chapter will be posted soon! :)

CHAPTER 18: What's In Store

D ARIUS

Throughout the entire plane ride over, I didn't want to explain to Variella exactly what was going on until we got to the safe house.

She however, decided that until I told her what was going on, she wasn't going to talk to me and honestly, I was going crazy.

When we finally arrived at our safe house, we settled into all of our rooms.

Since we were all feeling jet-lagged, Variella and I decided to take a nap in our room. Except before we did, she just laid on her side in the bed, turned away from me.

"Variella." I began.

"Unless you're explaining to me in what's going on, I have nothing ti say to you." She says.

"Fair enough. I will tell you what's going on but just hear me out please." I started.

It takes her a moment before she then turns over onto her other side, now with us facing one another.

"What?" She says.

"Larry, the guy I got in a fight with. He uh, he's not someone you really should ever double cross. He's hurt so many and is sick and twisted. Then the way he talked to you and looked at you, just promise me that no matter what, you will stay with me." I start to plead.

She looks at me now with a worried look and tears in her eyes.

"I told you already I would." She tells me.

"Larry is the one that got my ex girlfriend raped and murdered. He was the one who initiated it and I can't have that happen to you. I would never be able to forgive myself." I confess with tears feeling like they are about to fall down my face.

"Darius, it's okay." She says as she places her hand on the side of my face as we look into each other's eyes. "I'm not going anywhere and nobody's going to hurt me." She says.

I then touch the side of her face and rub my thumb gently on her cheek.

"Variella, I love you." I tell her.

"I love you too." She smiles back at me.

We kiss each other and make love before falling asleep in one another's arms.

Later on, we woke up around dinner time and when we opened up our eyes and saw each other, neither one of us needed to say anything because we both already knew we had ready said enough.

I never thought I would ever be able to say 'I love you' to anyone again since my ex and now that I did, I have so many mixed emotions right now.

Honestly I feel a little scared because she's got me hooked. More than I think I have ever been. I know this all might seem too sudden and too fast with the I love you's but I guess it really is true what they say about how the heart wants what the heart wants.

While walking downstairs to join everyone, we saw that the food my men had gone out to buy had just returned and were setting up the table.

While sitting and eating pizza, we all tried to think of stuff to talk about so that we could avoid any awkward silence but of course, I could tell everyone wanted to know about why we all up and left so fast.

"So, I'm just gonna say it..." Kix started. "What's going on?" He asks me.

"A few days ago, I discovered something. I might have made things a little worse by getting in a fight with Larry last night but, I had found that Blake works with him."

Then just like that, the room became dead silent and remained that way along with everybody surprised at what I just said. Then I see Variella who I can tell is about to have a panic attack and to be honest, this was exactly what I was worried about having happen but I have to tell her, all of them in what's to come.

Next chapter will be posted soon! :)

I wonder what it is and could be?!

CHAPTER 19: Still Need To Talk

V ARIELLA

I had to excuse myself and try to calm myself down. So I started heading upstairs and as I entered the room, I walked out onto the balcony outside of the room that overlooked the backyard and tried slowing down my breathing but the tears, I couldn't stop.

How could he have done what he did and then now we have to leave because of him losing his temper with that Larry guy only to find out he works with Blake?!?

I was deep in my thoughts that I hadn't realized Darius had come in until I heard him behind me.

"Variella?" He says.

I turn around and make sure he see's the tears.

"How could you not remember that small detail that the guy you flipped out on was associated with Blake? Why didn't you think about that before you released the 'tough guy' in you?!" I snapped at him.

He holds the bridge of his nose as he closes his eyes and lets out a sigh before looking back up at me.

"I know I fucked up. I'm a fuck up. And you know what? You don't make it easy for me. I told you before in who I am. You knew that before we got together. I mean shit, I've been busting my ass off trying so hard to make you happy. To become what you want me to be but you know what? I can't be that. I just can't!" He explains as he fires back at me.

"I'm not asking you to change who you are. I'm just wanting you to be the REAL Darius that I see. The one you're so afraid to be. Besides, who chased who, huh?! You're the one that would get so jealous that you would...." I started to rant but he stopped me by walking towards me with balled up fists by his sides.

"Just stop it!" He frustratingly snaps at me as he pulls at his hair. "You women are so fucking complicated. Not to mention UNREALISTIC!"

"What the hell is that supposed to mean?!" I asked crossing my arms over my chest.

"It means that you expect this prince charming type of guy who will come and rescue you and give you a peaceful life. You want the look of a bad boy but you want them to be nice on the inside. Well guess what? THAT is unrealistic!" He snaps at me.

"What are you saying? You want to break up with me?" I yell back at him.

"I don't know." He says.

I know we are fighting and maybe he is just saying it out of anger but at the same time, I can't help but feel hurt.

"Fine, let me do you a favor then and just get the hell out!" I scream at him.

When I stomp my way towards the door and he stops me by grabbing my wrist.

"You can't leave!" He scowls at me.

"Fuck you Darius! I'm done with you!" I yell at him while I try wriggling out from his grasp.

"Stop it!" He says.

I continue trying until he starts backing me up hard against the wall and holds my wrists above my head while looking at me.

"Let me go asshole!" I yell at him.

We both then stop for a moment before we have lust take over and the next thing I know, he smashes his lips onto mine.

At first I don't kiss him back but then I start to give in and feel him start to force his fingers down my pants and starts rubbing my clit making me moan into his mouth.

We start practically ripping each others clothes off until I feel him start to walk me over towards the bed where he immediately rolls on a condom and then thrusts deep and hard inside of me.

The thrusts become deeper and harder than the last as we kiss and both moan.

"I love you." He says between thrusts.

"I love you too." I reply between him thrusting inside of me.

"My god you feel so fucking good." He tells me.

"So do you. Please don't stop." I tell him.

He starts picking up the pace and looks into my eyes then places one of my nipples into his mouth hungrily before doing the same to the other one.

Then he stops and pulls out.

"Get on all fours." He demands and I have to say, I'm kind of liking this. It's almost like he's showing me how much he really is sorry and loves me. Not to mention how bad he wants me.

"Okay." I reply as I turn around and get on all fours while smacks my ass before thrusting himself inside of me again going deep and hard right away.

"Fuck!" I moan out loud.

He grabs my hair as he pounds away at me from behind causing nothing but pure pleasure.

"Shit baby, I'm gonna come." He moans out loud to me.

"Me too." I moan.

He thrusts deep inside me harder and harder a few more times before we both come at the same time.

I have to be honest, I know it's going to be hard for me to walk after this. That was AMAZING!!

We still need to talk but for now, we both need to rest.

Next chapter will be posted soon! :)

I know it was short of a racy scene but it was kind of spontaneous.

CHAPTER 20: Why This Life?!?

- -

D ARIUS

Alright, so I couldn't help but be turned on at the fact of her telling me off. However, at the same time, I know we still needed to talk about what's going on and what's going to happen also. Not to mention the fact that she has to admit that I did mean what I told her last night in that she already did know what I was like before she decided to date me and how I really have been trying to control my temper and everything just for her.

This morning when we woke up, we got ready and I told her that I was going to explain everything downstairs after breakfast in front of everyone so that we all can figure things out.

So after breakfast was over, we next headed into the living room and I started explaining.

"Okay, look, I know that I fucked up the other night when I fought Larry. But the truth is that I really didn't realize what I had done until afterwards. Which is why we're here now. I had found out days before that Blake and him were real good friends and were working with each other. Apparently,

Blake has been trying to get rid of me for years, along with Larry as we all know too. And it seems they have a plan to take me down." I start to explain.

"What do you mean, a plan? How did you find out?" Kix asks.

"Randy. The guy I use whenever we need to find someone. He even was able to record a conversation he overheard Larry and Blake were discussing while eating dinner together a couple weeks ago." I explain.

"What the hell?" Torrence says.

"I know. But now we're gonna have a big issue." I mention.

"Like what? What could be worse than that?" Torrence asks.

I look over at Variella who looks at me shocked and looks mad but like she's on the verge of tears as I give her a look of sympathy.

"Blake and Variella here, they used to date." I started.

"And let me guess, he wants her back?!" Morielle asks with her arms crossed over her chest and scowls at me.

"Yeah. But not like you think. Him and Larry have gone up the ranks in running their trafficking business and supposedly have mentioned in wanting Variella." I finish trying to hide the disgust I feel saying that.

The room falls silent and Variella looks shocked and then starts to fight back tears.

"Listen, more than anything, he wants her. So we need to focus on protecting her the best we can." I tell them all.

"You have got to be shitting me!" One of my guys says.

"What?!" I glared at him.

"First you don't tell us until now after we have up and left suddenly that we're being targeted by the two assholes we should have taken out a long time ago. And for what? HER?" He says with distaste in his voice and points at Variella.

"Watch it." I warn him through clenched teeth while the rest of the guys, including Morielle, Torrence and Kix all give him the same look as me warning him to shut the fuck up.

"This is bullshit and you know it! All for a fucking piece of ass!" He says and that's what made me snap.

I go up to him before he has a chance to respond and punch the shit out of him, knocking him back and causing him to break the coffee table before then picking him up by the collar and punching him even harder over and over again while on top of him.

"STOP IT!" I heard Morielle yell while Torrence and a few other guys pried me off of him.

"I swear if you ever talk about her like that I will fucking slit your throat you motherfucker! Now get the fuck out of my house and I mean it, NEVER fucking come back again unless you have your shit together or else you're wife will know what it's like to be a widow, I swear to god!" I threaten him before turning and looking at Variella who looks scared right now.

I start to leave out to the back to get some fresh air and cool off while everyone else takes care of the guy for me.

Once the sunlight hit my face along with the nice breeze, I started to calm down. Fuck, why did I have to choose this way of life? Why did everything have to be this way? Why couldn't I have had a normal childhood and had normal parents?!

Next chapter will be posted soon! :)

CHAPTER 21: No Matter What....I Love you

V ARIELLA

After everything that had just went down, I began feeling a huge wave of guilt for many different things. For one, about what all I said last night in the heat of the moment including the part about the fact he was right in that I did know what he was like when I decided to date him so I can't keep blaming him or using that as an excuse.

Then after what all he had just said and did because of me and because of Blake. I can't help but feel like all of this is my fault because clearly it has to be since now we are all being targeted on account that Blake wants me back so he can sell me to some sick fuck to become a victim in his and Larry's trafficking business.

This lifestyle is somewhat like the movies but mostly not. Which I never necessarily compared it to any of those but it really is a lot harder than I thought.

Right in this moment however, I really feel bad about Darius and how he's feeling right now. So while all the guys start picking up the guy that made that comment to me and everything, I made my way out to the backyard and walked up to Darius.

"Darius?" I say quietly.

He turns around and I see tears begin falling down his face.

"I'm so fucking sorry Variella. You were right last night. I'm a monster with a really bad temper and I have involved you in a lifestyle you don't deserve. I thought I could handle it and be okay with involving you in my life and everything that comes with it but, I just can't. It isn't right and it isn't fair neither." He tells me through sniffles.

I walk up to him and hold his face so he's looking into my eyes.

"Look at me." I tell him. "I love you. We love each other. I knew what I was getting myself into before I said yes to being your girl and I don't regret that one bit. I never will. And rather or not you and I are together, I unfortunately would have had to always deal with Blakc and always look over my shoulder for the rest of my life to make sure he never came for me. I've always known deep down what kind of person he was. HE is a monster, not you. And there is nowhere else I'd rather be than here with all of you, but especially you." I assure him.

He holds my face and leans his forehead forward touching mine and we close our eyes as we share an amazingly intimate moment together before kissing me passionately and long.

After we finished talking, we headed back inside with the both of us feeling better and everyone seemed to be scattered all around the house doing their own thing almost as if nothing happened. But Morielle, Torrence and Kix all waited for us.

"Are you good?" Morielle asks him.

"Yeah." Darius nods.

"Cool. Then we can figure out a plan to take these assholes down once and for all." Torrence says. "But you really need to tell us things that are going on."

"I promise." Darius assures them.

"Good. Well, let's just relax for now and then think up of something later." Kix mentions. "Oh and by the way, it's about time you told that asshole off. He's been such a pain in the ass since the day he joined." He says.

"I know." Darius rolled his eyes.

Everyone started going off to do their own thing after we agreed to all meet up tonight to come up with a plan.

Darius looks at me for a moment and while we look into each other's eyes, I feel we are having a moment that I only heard about in books and seen in movies. I'm actually experiencing a moment where everything around us disappears. I know it sounds cliche and what not but, it does exist and it feels amazing.

Then he gently tucks a hair behind my ear before placing his hand on the side of my face.

"I want to take you somewhere that nobody else knows about but me." He tells me.

"Okay." I nod.

We both get ready and we head out the backyard and through the many trees that isn't the amount you would have in the woods but enough to have privacy for a couple miles worth.

I'm not sure where we were going but I can say that either way, I do trust him.

Next chapter will be posted soon! :)

CHAPTER 22: What Has This Woman Done To Me!?

D ARIUS

I need to really earn her trust and to make sure she knows without a doubt just how much I love her and care by showing her a place I have never shown anyone before. It's what I call my safe place and that I discovered when I was a little kid.

We walked a mile or so in through the trees until we came to a clearing where it had beautiful grass all around and trees that provided the utmost shade.

It was peaceful. Only I knew about it. And now, the biggest secret of all, I am about to show to someone I love.

"This is nice." I hear her say. "It seems very peaceful. Almost like what you'd see in a movie." She smiled.

"I brought you here because I know that so much is going on right now and that you're probably questioning me and you and...." I stop as soon as I hear her cut me off.

"Darius..." She starts but I stop her.

"Please, let me finish. This place is somewhere I found as a kid and used to go to whenever I heard my parents fighting or something bad happened at school and felt like I had nobody to turn to. This was my safe place. I could think here. I could dream. I could do whatever." I started to explain.

"I wanted you to see this so that whenever you doubt us or anything, I want you to remember this place. I want this to be our place. You're the only other person that knows about this. And I thought if I'd show you it, you'd see just how much I really do care about and love you." I tell him.

She looks like she is on the verge of tears and has a look on her face that I can't tell if rather or not it's good tears or bad.

Next I feel her grab hold of my face and leans in to kiss me before moving her head back a little and placing her forehead against mine.

"Thank you for showing me this place. I love you too." She says.

That just made me feel better and relieved. Because showing her this place meant a lot and the fact she understood that so quickly, it's amazing.

We stay there for a few hours and talk with each other until we begin heading on back towards the house where the guys are all hanging out waiting for us to return.

Torrence, Kix, Morielle and I along with a few other guys in my crew all sat at the dining room table and started trying to over a plan while Variella was sitting beside me.

I preferred her being on my lap, but she insisted on sitting in her own chair.

"Before we do anything, we're gonna have to find a way into Larry's place. Him and Blake have been staying together at that big mansion over on Shadow Hills. Their security is really good so we have to find a way to get in without being detected." I started.

"Pff." Torrence scoffs. "Yeah, that's not gonna happen. There is no way we can go undetected. I mean, we're all great at what we do but when it comes to going against Larry? He's already thought of all this."

"Then how do you suggest we do this?" I asked.

"I don't know but, there's no way we can just sneek in. He'll have the whole place surrounded by his men." Torrence mentions.

"I might know a way to get in." Variella interrupts.

"How?" I asked curious.

"There's a hidden tunnel or something underneath the mansion. I remember accidentally stumbling across it when I stayed the night over there once and couldn't remember where the room was at." She says.

"How do you know for sure that it wasn't just a cellar or nothing?" I asked.

"I opened the latch out of curiosity the next day when Blake and them had to go to 'work'. It's really long but, I noticed there were other doors built into the flooring on the first floor in certain places and I think they lead to certain rooms." She finishes.

We all look at each other in shock but we all are very impressed by her knowing that.

"Good job, baby." I smile and wink at her.

"Thanks." She smiles back at me.

"Great then, we just need to tell the other guys and get ourselves ready tomorrow." I said.

We all got up and left the room to head to our bedrooms and as soon as me and Variella headed into the bedroom, we made love to each other and as she fell asleep with her head on my chest, cuddling, I couldn't help but start to worry about what could happen to me. What could happen to her.

This has to be the last time I do something like this. In fact, after this is over, I'm gonna take enough money to leave and live a nice comfortable life. Just her and I. She deserves a better life and I'm sure I can open up a business somewhere.

What has this woman done to me!?

Next chapter will be posted soon! :)

CHAPTER 23: I Messed Up

V ARIELLA

I hope that Darius doesn't think I'm gonna just stay back and let him have all the fun. Not to mention that I have to show them what all I was talking about with the tunnel underground.

He was downstairs talking with his men about the plan for tonight when they stopped and all looked at me with a smile.

"What?" I asked them.

"Nothing." Darius smiles at me. "In fact, wee were just going over the plans for the big fight tomorrow night. I was able to even set up a fake meeting with Larry." He says.

"Why?" I asked curious.

"Because I know he isn't stupid. He'll never suspect that my guys will be underneath." He replies.

"Okay..." I replied. "So then where will I be at?" I asked.

"You're staying here." Darius tells me.

"Oh hell no. The tunnel was my idea and I'm going to!" I say with authority as I place my hands on my hips.

"Uh oh." Morielle says.

"No, you're not. I already told you before that you're not going so drop it." Darius fires back at me with a glare.

"Why the hell not? And when in the hell did we talk about me not going? You may have said you didn't want me to but that isn't necessarily discussing it." I snap back at him.

"Variella, I'm not going to repeat myself." He says through clenched teeth.

"Well you don't get to tell me what to do!" I tell him. "Besides, you can't leave me behind. We both know that Blake could easily be setting you all up. While you're having a meeting with Larry, Blake could easily be using that opportunity in finding a way to get to me." I tell him.

I can tell by the look on everybody's face that they are starting to feel uncomfortable.

"He won't!" He says.

"He could! You need to stop and let go of what happened in your past! I'm not her!" I snap at him not meaning to bring it up or say it the way that I just now did but it just came out.

The moment it came out, everybody looked at Darius and then at me with looks of pity but also, that I shouldn't have said that.

I try and walk up to him and start to try and apologize.

"Darius I'm sorry." I try and say while about to touch his shoulder but I flinch and quickly pull my hand back as soon as he swats it and stands up abruptly before forcefully pushing his chair back.

"You know what? You want to fucking kill yourself then go ahead! Sorry for ever fucking care about your ass. And who knows, maybe deep down you want Blake to come for you." He says with so much anger.

As much as I deserved something like that, it still hurt. I tried fighting back the tears that were about to fall down my face as I look into his eyes.

He looks at me with disgust and so much anger then moves passed me and leaves to go for a ride while slamming the door behind him.

I felt embarrassed. I almost felt as though I was a kid that was just yelled out by their dad in front of family or friends. Then I felt disgusted with myself and even more upset though that he never let me explain to him in what I meant.

Although, this is really all my fault. I should have known better. I never should have said what I did. Now he's pissed and gone.

"Variella..." I heard Morielle say to me.

"I'm so sorry guys. I'm sorry for everything." I started to cry and quickly ran towards the bedroom upstairs closing the door behind me.

I laid in bed sobbing really hard as I may have lost the best thing in my life. I'm such an idiot.

After almost two hours of crying, I finally had nothing left to cry out and after realizing that Darius hadn't come home yet, I decided to just take a shower instead.

So I headed into the bathroom and turned music on using my phone and then grabbed some PJ's before moving the shower curtain over and suddenly jumping back as soon as I see Blake and he is grinning in a sinister way that I recognized him always doing before he would do something bad.

So I turn and try to scream but he yanks me back by my hair and slams my head, face first into the mirror, breaking the mirror into a million pieces and knocking me out. Darkness consumed me so fast, I had no idea what happened.

Next chapter will be posted soon! :)

CHAPTER 24: Worst Nightmare

D ARIUS

I can't believe she just said all of that. I never thought she would ever use my ex in that way.

Then again I said things too that I'm not too proud of neither.

What the hell am I doing now? I'm just driving pissed off and meanwhile, I feel guilty and terrible for what just happened and for me just leaving instead of staying behind for her and I to talk things out.

Although with the way that I feel right now, I can't even look at her.

So I start to go to a place that I haven't been to in a while but that I know I need to. In order for me to have closure for good on my past and to do right with my future and Variella, I need to do this.

I pulled up and there were very few people here it seemed. Which was good. I needed the peace and quiet.

I walked up to the headstone that read 'Mary Featherson'. I kneel down and start to tear up as I remember the last time I saw her body after she was found. The coroner had to use her teeth to identify it was her.

"Hey Mare. I haven't been here in a while and need to tell you something. I'm scared right now. I'm so fucking scared that I don't know what to do. I feel like I'm fucking up no matter how hard I try and make things better. Worst of all, I keep fucking up with Variella. In the beginning, it was really hard for me to even let another person inside without thinking about you because she gave me the same feelings as you did. Is that wrong? She makes me laugh the way you do, makes me smile, makes me happy in general but most of all, makes me want to be a better man. She see's past all the bad stuff with me, just like you did."

I stop myself for a moment to wipe my tears.

"I'm so sorry. I shouldn't have left you. I should have tried harder to get you back. You should be alive right now, not me. You were a great person always. Not me." I begin crying even more.

"I'm in love with Variella. I just fucked up with her and I need your advice on what to do. I miss you so fucking much." I start to cry even more and harder than before.

I start to hear my phone go off and when I look down at the number it says it's 'unknown'. Those kind of numbers I never answer. So I ignore it and put the phone back in my pocket before continuing.

"I know I need to change my ways but it's really hard. I've even forgave my father for ever starting me in all of this because you told me to. Now though..." I was interrupted by my phone going off again.

I was frustrated this time as I saw it was from an 'Unknown' number again. This time whoever it was was going to get it.

"What?!" I answered pissed off.

"You really should learn to answer quicker." I heard Blake's voice tell me.

"What the hell do you want?" I asked through clenched teeth.

"I've got something of yours that I think you might want back." He says and then the next voice I hear is a scared shaken up Variella.

"D-Darius?" She says.

"Variella? Baby are you okay?" I ask.

"Aww isn't that sweet. You two are in love. It's too bad that you guys couldn't work things out. You both made such a cute couple." He starts to taunt.

"I swear to god if you..." I started to threaten him until he stopped.

"Tsk tsk tsk. Now that's no way to talk to the man who holds the very thing that's most valuable to him. I would hate to see your new girlfriend here get the same treatment as your little Mary. Boy did she put up a fight." He says with an evil chuckle.

"I swear to you that I will kill you and I will do it slowly." I promise him.

"We'll see. First, let's see what all you are willing to do for this one and if you can get to her on time." He says.

"What do I have to do?" I asked.

"I'll message you an address. Meet me there tomorrow night and we'll settle the score between you and me once and for all." He says.

"And what does Larry say?" I asked.

"Aww, you didn't here? He had an accident. The poor fucker just couldn't CUT it." He says with a lot of emphasis on the word 'cut'.

"You're a sick fuck." I tell him.

"Yes I am. Now that you know that, I'm sure you won't be wasting any time in getting your guys together to meet me and my crew." He says.

"We'll be there." I tell him.

"Good boy. Now, be sure to tell your people, no hard feelings." He says before he hangs up.

I immediately try and call Morielle and she doesn't answer so I try and call Torrence who eventually answers as soon as I get into the car and began heading back to the house as fast as I could, running through all the red lights.

When I finally arrived at the house and ran inside, I noticed things were broken and scattered all over the place, most of my guys were icing their wounds as Morielle explained to me about what happened with the ambush.

I then explained everything in what we needed to do tomorrow night and everyone got on board and began preparing before we then eventually went to bed.

Although I couldn't sleep in the bed alone knowing she was taken.

Tonight I'd sleep alone but tomorrow night, she'll be right by my side.

I ended up sleeping in one of the extra spare bedrooms after Morielle had begun sweeping up the mirror pieces shattered all over the bathroom floor along with the blood from Variella.

I knew I'd have nightmares tonight of my own but tomorrow, I will be Blake's worst fucking nightmare.

Next chapter will be posted soon! :)

CHAPTER 25: F*** You!!

V ARIELLA

I woke up with a really bad pain in the front part of my head and grabbed it as I felt it make the rest of my head start to throb and become quickly almost unbearable.

Then as I opened and adjusted my eyes a little more and took a look around, I noticed I was in a disgustingly dirty and grotesque room.

While looking around, I then hear a door open from not too far away and see a couple of men come walking in with one carrying a bowl of something along with a glass of water.

"Here." He says as he tosses the bowl towards me and it looks unappetizing, almost as though it was old oatmeal.

"Where am I? What's going on?" I asked.

"You'll find out soon enough. In the meantime, eat up." He says before leaving while the other guy who walked down here with him took a seat in one of the chairs close by to the cell I was in.

"Why are you doing this?" I asked.

"I'm not doing this to you." The guy replies without making eye contact as he lights up a cigarette.

"Blake." I say under my breath.

"You should really eat." He says before blowing out smoke and sitting back watching me.

"I'm not hungry." I lie as my stomach begins to growl.

"Sure. But you see Princess, it ain't up to you. Blake wants you to eat up." He says before taking a drag from his cigarette.

"Why?" I asked.

"Because, we can't necessarily starve you to death before your soon-to-be owner, comes and collects you. Although you could stand to lose some weight so he can enjoy you even more but I guess some like the fatty's." He smirks.

"You're lying. Besides, where is Larry? Why isn't he down here?" I ask.

"Because Larry has been disposed of." He says.

"I don't believe this." I say under my breath.

"Aww don't be so sad. I'm sure this guy will be good to you." He says with an evil grin.

"Fuck you." I glare at him before then picking up the bowl of slop, as I'm calling it and I throw it at him along with the water right after and he quickly stands up then puts out his cigarette and stomps over towards the cell.

"Fucking bitch!" He says.

He starts to unlock the cell door and comes up and kneels down in front of me and hits me across the face.

"You fucking fat ugly whore!" He yells as he hits me again before getting on top of me.

"Asshole get the fuck off of me!" I yell back at him while struggling to do anything with my rope tied up hands and then finally somebody thankfully comes down and stops him.

Which was perfect as I grabbed his switchblade knife he had hanging half out of his pocket and quickly put it in my bra before he looks back at me.

"Hey, Blake wants to see you." The guy says.

"I'll be back fucking slut." He says before slapping me hard again.

Then he stands up and after locking the cell door, he leaves with the guy. Then as soon as I hear the door close, I take the knife and open it up and start to try and untie the rope around my ankles before trying to free my wrists and though it took me longer, it still worked and then now it was moving onto the cell door and trying to pick the lock.

It's really hard and tricky with the knife but I did read somewhere that it can be done.

I try to unlock it and right when I feel as though I finally have it, I hear the door from upstairs open up and down comes that asshole again looking more pissed off but with a smile also as he starts opening the door while I sit back against the wall until he gets close enough for me to jam the knife into his neck and start twisting it, making sure the wound doesn't close.

He yells in pain while grabbing the knife and falling to the ground while I grab the gun from the back of his pants and begin to slowly and cautiously make my way up the stairs.

Next chapter will be posted soon! :)

CHAPTER 26: What The Hell?!?

D ARIUS

We were finishing up getting prepared before we headed over to Larry's and Blake's house.

I was putting the last weapon I armed myself with into the back of my pants when I heard a knock on the door.

"Hey, we're all ready to go downstairs." Morielle says.

"Okay. I'll be down in a minute." I tell her as I sit for a moment on the bed thinking about a few things.

"You alright?" She asks while walking over and sitting down beside me.

"I shouldn't have left. I swore that this time around, I'd protect her. Who knows if she's even still alive." I begin to say while choking back on some tears.

"Again, it isn't your fault. This would have happened rather you were here or not. And do you honestly think that Mary would want you to feel guilty?" Morielle asks.

"No." I reply. "I went to see her earlier. That's where I went to before this all happened."

"How'd it go?" She asks me.

"Pretty good actually. I was finally able to close that chapter in my life and then asked her what I should do. Then I got the call."

"She always did have perfect timing." She tells me causing me to laugh.

"Yeah, she did." I reply through sniffles.

"Thanks for always putting up with me and for bringing Variella into my life." I tell her.

"Hey, Variella was all Mary but as far as always putting up with your stubborn ass, yeah, you never did make it easy." She winks and smiles at me.

We both share a good laugh together before Kix comes walking in interrupting us.

"Hey! We gonna go kick some ass while rescuing your woman or what?" He says.

"We're coming." Morielle tells him.

Everyone's already in their cars outside waiting for us as we start heading out there and taking off.

While on our way, I began to focus even more than ever before on that I had only one goal. That was to get back Variella and get the hell out of there.

After dropping most of the guys off in the very back to go through the underground tunnel, Torrence, Morielle, Kix and I had all gone around the sides and the back while joining a few of my other guys as some were sent to go around towards the back of the house and try to sneak in there while I was going to take the front.

I took in a deep breath before starting to run towards the house, shooting anybody that got in my way and who wasn't one of my guys.

There were only four out tonight and as soon as I shot the last one, I busted open the front door with my gun still drawn and a few of Blake's and Larry's guys tried shooting at me but I was able to dive behind the couch before then starting to shoot back at them and then I heard Torrence and them come running in.

"Boss, you okay?" Torrence asks.

"I'm fine. Go find Variella while I go look for Blake." I tell them.

"Alright." Torrence says and they all start to leave, heading upstairs.

I begin cautiously taking strides around the house, looking around every corner and in every room.

Next I began making my way down towards the long hallway as I heard my guys upstairs moving around and could hear guns going odd along with grunts from pain as I hear them also start fighting.

While walking down this long dark hallway, I start to hear movement coming from a nearby room and once I open the door slowly and look around to make sure no one will jump out at me from anywhere while I check it out, I walk inside.

Slowly I continue moving around the room, looking underneath the bed, behind the long window curtain that barely touches the floor. Then I hear moving around in the bathroom.

I get a little more nervous before I finally open the door and right away I see a bloodied up Variella trying to attack me with her fists.

"No! Don't fucking touch me!" She screams not realizing it's me.

However, I quickly push her up against the wall and cover her mouth so she can see that it's me.

"Shh. It's me." I tell her while looking into her eyes.

Quickly I begin to notice that the blood on both her clothes and the rest of her is more of others than of her own.

"Darius?" She cries.

"Yeah. It's me baby." I tell her while trying to wipe tears from her eyes.

"I didn't think you'd come for me. I'm so sorry." She cries into my chest.

"No Variella. I'm the one that's sorry. But babe, we need to get the fuck out of here." I tell her.

She nods her head in agreement and grabs some kitchen knife that I notice her picking up from the bathroom sink and am grateful she didn't try to stab me with it

She stays close behind me as we slowly make our way out into the hallway with my gun drawn again and then out of nowhere, I hear a muffled screaming coming from behind me and as soon as I turn around, I am knocked out.

Next chapter will be posted soon! :)

CHAPTER 27: Sick & Twisted

V ARIELLA

I was more than happy and excited that Darius had come for me and then found me. I hadn't been in the bathroom for too long before he had found me and now, right when I thought we were gonna be able to leave and not worry about Blake or anyone stopping us, I felt two arms grab me from behind and immediately I started screaming but then I saw one of Blake's guys then knock out Darius causing him to fall and caught him before he hit the floor and started to carry him away along with me.

The guy that had me in his grasp, hit me really hard across the face and caused me to become real dizzy so he then picked me up and carried me down the stairs.

Which he had to have been strong as the hulk or something because of him being able to pick me up and carry me without a problem.

Once I finally came to, I felt myself being set onto my feet on the ground and was just coming to and no longer being dizzy anymore.

Then I saw Darius along with Kix, Torrence and Morielle all tied up and beaten badly as they seemed to have been tied to the chairs.

Next I feel myself being forced to sit down onto a chair facing all of them, having both my wrists rope tied behind my back and then my ankles being zip tied to the chair legs.

"You're such a fucking asshole Blake!" I tell him as I see the guy that carried in Darius begins tying him up.

"I'm not the enemy here sweetheart. At least I had been honest with you in who I was." Blake starts to say as he walks over in front of me and kneels down.

"The hell you were. You took me to that party and tried to fucking whore me out." I remind him.

"Well, besides that, which I eventually would have told you but you just couldn't wait. But as far as everything else, you were just too blind and stupid to see the real me. I never hid myself. You saw what you wanted to see." He says.

"You're so fucking stupid. You never..." I began but he got up and grabbed my face harshly forcing me to look up at him.

"Let's refresh your memory, shall we?" He asks.

"What are you doing?" I asked as he just stands there smirking at me.

"Do you remember that night when I took you to that steakhouse for dinner and you went off to use the restroom and then came back and noticed I was doing a deal then and there with one of the waiters? Giving him some cash along with a packet of drugs?" He asks with a cocked eyebrow.

"No." I tell him then wince as he squeezes my face tighter.

"Bullshit! You fucking remember. You saw what I did and still you refused to see it. Then there was the day when I picked you up from work and then we had ran some of my errands. Those manila envelopes, obviously you could tell there was lots of cash in them. Not to mention the packets I had you hand me sometimes. That wasn't salt." He states.

"Okay fine. Maybe I did choose to ignore it. But that's still no excuse for anything you have done!" I exclaimed before spitting in his face which made Morielle, Kix and Torrence laugh a little bit.

The men with guns held against their heads and cocked them making them all shut up.

Blake chuckles in a sinister way also and takes out his handkerchief and wipes it off after removing his grip and slapping me hard.

"You see? You always knew." He laughs.

Then I look up and hear Darius groaning and wince as he starts to open his eyes and finally wake up.

I next wince as I feel Blake yank my hair back harshly and forces me to look at all of my friends and Darius. Then lets go of me and has one of his men put a gun up to my head and then has the guy who carried Darius and tied him to the chair, yank on his hair and forces him to look at me.

"We're gonna play a game guys. Who likes games as much as I do?" Blake asks.

I swear he is so twisted and sick.

Next chapter will be posted soon! :)

CHAPTER 28: I Swear.....

D ARIUS

As I started opening my eyes a little more and realizing what was going on, I felt my head being yanked back by some asshole while pointing a gun up to the side of my head, forcing me to look at Variella that is sitting across form us with a gun to her head as well while Blake mentions something about playing a game.

"Alright now, here are the rules in how the game is to be played." Blake starts with far too much amusement in the tone of his voice then there should be.

"Why don't you just get down to what the fuck you want to do with us." I challenged him, calling his bluff whilst trying to distract him.

"Aww, but I wanted to play a game. Trust me, you all will have a lot of fun. Or at least I will. It is one of my favorite games." He grins in a sinister way.

I look at Variella who is crying silently really hard while looking as though she telling me at the same time in her eyes she is sorry. As I do the same as well with mine towards her and my friends who all have just now had duct tape put over their mouths.

"Now, I'm going to ask you several questions here Darius and if you get them right, then, you get a prize. But if you get them wrong..." He begins to say before squatting beside Variella and rubbing the back of her neck then tightening his grip on her before continuing.

"But if you get them wrong, then this little, or should I say big disgusting thing, will be hurt. If by the end you have more right questions wrong, then I will just request a tiny amount of money from you and let all of you go and that's that." He says.

I glare it him for a few moments before I finally agree to it. Plus, what other choice do I really have?!

"Fine." I agree.

"Good. First question.....A few years back, you made a deal with several big clients that were once Larry's. Did you intentionally try and take them away from him?" He asks.

"No." I tell him thinking it's a stupid question. "I had no idea that he even did business with them as they had not told me." I answered.

He looks at me for a moment deciding if rather or not I was telling the truth.

"Alright. Next question....Did you ever know that Larry and I were related?" He asks me with a cocked eybrow.

"No." I reply.

"Tsk tsk tsk. That's a shame." He says and then pulls out his pocket switch-blade knife and then places it against Variella's skin near her neck and start to drag it along her skin causing her to scream and bleed.

The man with a gun to her head covers her mouth.

"No! I want them all to hear her scream." Blake snaps at the guy.

"I swear I'm gonna fucking kill you." I warn him.

"Hey, you should have a have answered honestly." He tells me.

"Fine then, yes, I knew." I confessed never having told anyone I knew before.

"It's too late now for that." He smirks in satisfaction. "Now, lets continue. While dating my sister, did you for once ever think about the retaliation and consequences for that?" He asks.

"You son-of-a-bitch." I tell him.

"What? Doesn't your crew know? Does Variella know?" He asks.

"Don't." I tell him.

"You see, Variella and friends of Darius, his ex, Mary, was my little sister and you got her killed." He states.

"It wasn't my fault and you fucking know it." I remind him with a scowl.

"Bullshit! Larry told me everything that happened and said that YOU ordered the hit and allowed those men to assault her and then kill her and dump her body as if she was a nobody." He exclaims.

"It wasn't me. It was Larry and his guys. He tried getting to me by getting her and I swear to god it wasn't my fault." I start to plead.

"I don't believe you. In fact, let's make that the final question. You'll clearly never tell me the truth for anything and well, frankly I'm starting to get bored." He says and then looks at the guy with a gun to Variella's head and nods.

The guy grins and then starts to remove Variella from the chair with her wrists still tied as he throws her over his shoulder while she kicks and screams then walks out with her.

"You motherfucker! I swear to god I'm gonna kill you and your men!" I yell out at him as I struggle and wriggle around trying hard to get up and out of the chairs along with Morielle and them trying to do the same as they also try to scream through the duct tape.

"Don't worry, I'll make sure you say goodbye this time before we finish her." Blake laughs in an evil way.

"I swear to..." I begin to say but duct tape is then put over my mouth and right away, I feel the guy that had the gun to my head start throwing blows from every angle to my face as did the other men with Morielle and the others.

Next chapter will be posted soon! :)

CHAPTER 29: The Last Time

V ARIELLA

This asshole carrying me up the stairs may be strong enough to carry me but meanwhile, I'm trying to think of a way to prevent him or any one of Blake's men trying to do anything to me. Suddenly I realize that I have to save my energy also if I had planned to try something once inside the place he was going to take me to.

He opens the door to some nice bedroom that's decently decorated and as soon as he kicks the door closed with his foot, he throws me onto the bed causing me to bounce up off of it a little bit and as I face him and prop myself onto my elbows, I start looking around for something to hit him over the head with or something.

I quickly try to reach over for the inn table's lamp while he unbuckles his pants and I suddenly feel my hand being squeezed tightly causing me to yelp in pain.

Before climbing on top of me, pinning me down and I struggle and try to kick him in between his legs but his weight is too heavy as he pins my legs down with his and has both my arms pinned above my head. .

"You like it rough huh?" Well that's good. Because so do me and all the other guys." He grins and tries to kiss me and I turn my head away but he grabs my face and squeezes tightly, forcing me to look at him.

"Not so fast. Now you better play nicely before I get the other guys to come in and join the fun all at once. Unless you like that?" He suggestively asks.

"Fuck you!" I tell him.

"Oh don't worry, we will." He tells me.

I try screaming loudly for help and the next thing I feel is a hard slap on my face as he still has my wrists pinned above my head with one hand while the other is trying to undo his buckle and zipper.

Finally he gets close enough and I bite down onto his mouth really hard causing him to yell out in pain and hold his mouth while I push him off finally and get the chance to kick him between his legs and get up while spitting out blood.

The door then bursts open and in walks a few more of Blake's men who I right away go to grab the lamp and yank it out of the socket then forcefully throw it at one of the guys (which isn't as easy when your hands are still tied together), luckily though, the impact caused a few pieces to shatter and had gotten into his eye while the other guys seemed to still come at me and grab me real quick then throw me onto the bed as one holds my hands down above my head again, then the other two hold apart my legs then I see Blake start to climb on top of me while starting to unbuckle his belt and I thought this was it.

Then suddenly the room fell silent as I next heard guns going off and the men holding me down along with the one on top of me had all been shot in the head.

Blake collapses on top of me and I start to scream while crying as his blood got all over me. Then I notice his body starting to roll off and there to pull me up by my tied wrists, was Darius. He held me so close.

"Are you alright baby?" He asks as he gives me a kiss and holds the back of my head.

"Yes." I nod my head.

He then cuts off the rope and we start to run out of the room with a few more gunshots going off downstairs and somehow, not sure how, but somehow, most of us were able to leave.

The moment we got outside though we were forced to come to a complete stop the moment we saw a lot of guns drawn and pointed at us from all these policemen.

They were all yelling at us to get down and to drop our weapons. Which we did.

All I could hear from Darius was him telling me in how sorry he was for everything as they handcuffed us all after they held us to the ground like WE were the damn criminals.

We were in questioning for hours and it even ended up lasting for a couple of days to get all of our statements.

For the most part, we all were let off. Since it was all in self defense mostly. However, Darius and his crew needed to pay for being involved in that kind of business anyways and for things they did in the past.

Though they all be let out early due to good behavior. Except me, I wasn't charged. Darius helped me and testified that I had nothing to do with any of it. That I was just a victim.

I was told by one of the detectives that he took a deal. It was a deal that broke my heart and his. A deal that I had to forever live with. A deal that made him and I not be able to be together or hear from each other ever again.

He told them he would testify against all the big leaders and that in exchange, he would have to go under a different identity and be in the Witness Protection Program.

I knew why he did it but it still hurt. My heart died the day I said goodbye. We told each other we loved one another always and forever, for the last time.

The End!

Milton Keynes UK
Ingram Content Group UK Ltd.
UKHW032032191024
449814UK00010B/611

9 798330 471416